MORE THAN YOU KNOW

The room became silent again.

Jairo continued. "I hope that bringing you here to Rio under these circumstances will make amends for such an unforgivable oversight. And since I am scheduled to be here until you leave, I hope, despite my business schedule, we can still spend some time together."

Mara felt as if she would drown in his eyes. "I'd like that."

"Now," Jairo pulled her to him, "come to me. Let me hug you. I want to feel you, Mara." He spoke his actions. "Let me lay my head against your hair. I am glad that you are here. You are a special woman. I hope you know that. Any woman who could dance the samba in her own unique way, like you did, and transform into a businesswoman of such professionalism is special in her own right. But you are also special because of what I believe your heart is capable of."

Eboni Snoe

More Than You Know

ARABESQUE

BET BOOKS

BET Publications, LLC
http://www.bet.com
http://www.arabesquebooks.com

ARABESQUE BOOKS are published by

BET Publications, LLC
c/o BET BOOKS
One BET Plaza
1900 W Place NE
Washington, DC 20018-1211

All Kensington Titles, Imprints, and Distributed Lines
are available at special quantity discounts for bulk pur-
chases for sales promotions, premiums, fund-raising,
and educational or institutional use. Special book ex-
cerpts or customized printings can also be created to fit
specific needs. For details, write or phone the office of
the Kensington special sales manager: Kensington Publishing Corp., 850 Third Avenue, New York, NY 10022,
attn: Special Sales Department, Phone: 1-800-221-2647.

First Printing: August 2004
10 9 8 7 6 5 4 3 2 1

Printed in the United States of America

1984 . . .

Mara Scott smiled and jumped off her bed. Happy, she skipped down the hall toward the kitchen where her mother waited.

"Mara, what were you doing? I've been calling you for five minutes."

"I was just thinking, that's all," Mara replied.

"Thinking about what?"

"Well, you said, you and Dad, if you have the money, you might buy me a new bicycle, and I was thinking about what it's going to look like." Her face beamed. "I could see myself riding it, and how that girl who doesn't like me was so jealous. She tried to push me down as I rode by, but I was too fast for her and—"

"Mara!" Janet knelt down and with wet hands took a hold of her. "You do more daydreaming than anybody I know, and honey, I don't want you to get caught up in a dream world. You're always daydreaming." She stood up and began to wash dishes again.

"Mommy it's not really daydreaming." She explained. "I sit down and think about things and then I see them. They come alive."

Janet looked at her. "It's good to have an imagination, Mara, because that means you are very creative. But you have to be careful not to get so caught up in it. There is a real world out here, sweetie, and you're old enough now, at eight, to accept that. There's a difference, Mara, between make-believe and reality. And I think you tend to spend more time than you should in the world of make-believe."

Mara's face fell. "But, Mommy, it's not that I'm trying to do it all the time. It just happens."

Janet placed her hands on Mara's shoulders. "Mara, do you know what reputation means?"

Mara shook her head.

"A reputation is what people believe about you, what they say about you. A person develops a reputation by what they say and do. So you have to be careful, Mara, in building your reputation because your reputation is very important in life. You don't want to say things that people can't count on." Janet smiled slightly. "Don't depend on a dream world, honey. You're smart enough, bright enough, to deal with life head-on. You don't have to dream your life away. A girl like you can do whatever she wants. She doesn't have to depend on unimportant things like looks, and she doesn't have to settle. You've got it up here, Mara." Janet tapped her index finger against her temple. "Use it, and never forget what Mommy has just told you."

Mara looked into her mother's sincere eyes. "Okay, Mommy. I won't."

Chapter 1

Mara climbed the stairs of her childhood home. She was glad the workday was done. It had been extremely busy, and Mara couldn't wait to lie in her bed and rest, if just for a little while. When she reached her bedroom, there was a note taped to the door. "I've gone to get new tires. Dad."

Mara removed her shoes and lay on the bed. She closed her eyes, but her mind refused to let go of work. She rehashed some office meetings, and Mara felt pleased about the design the local design team had agreed on for a Brazilian project. It hadn't been an easy task.

The telephone rang.

Mara opened her eyes and rolled onto her side. She picked up the phone. "Hello."

"Hey, Mara."

She smiled. "Hi, James. How are you?" Mara lay on her back.

"I'm doing okay."

"I didn't expect you to call so soon."

"I took off from work a little early today. I need to see you. As a matter of fact, I'm on my way over to pick you up now."

Mara's brow creased. "Okay. Are you thinking about getting some dinner?"

"Yes. Yes, definitely, we will eat and, uh . . . Mara . . . I just . . . You know we've been seeing each other for quite awhile, and neither one of us is getting any younger."

Mara sat up. "That's true."

"And I think we need to address that. I'm on my way."

She looked at the receiver. "I'll be ready."

Mara hung up the phone and lay on her back again. "What's going on with him? What could be so important that James can't wait to talk to me?" Mara squinted. "He sounded so serious." Her heart beat a little faster. "And did I hear him right? He said we've been seeing each other for a while, and we aren't getting any younger. My goodness." She closed her eyes and put her hands over them. "Oh my God, I wonder if James thinks it's time for us to get married?" A smile spread across her face. Although James was not the love of her life, he was a good, steady man. And Mara believed life with James would be secure with no surprises. They could have a good, simple life together. She sighed. With James there would be no unpaid bills, no drunken binges, and no women on the side. Some people might call their relationship dull, but Mara considered it safe. She smiled again.

Mara could see James get out of his car, walk up her sidewalk and ring the doorbell. Then the image changed. Mara saw James driving. Suddenly, she saw herself in the car as well, and James reached out and held her hand as he continued to drive.

"What is it, James? Tell me."

"I'm not going to tell you now. I want us to get to the restaurant, get comfortable, and then we'll talk."

"You know you're making me nervous with all this secrecy," Mara replied.

"There's nothing to be nervous about." He squeezed her hand. "Nothing at all."

They stopped in front of a beautiful restaurant that was unfamiliar to her.

"I brought a client to this place a couple of weeks ago," James said as they parked. "And I couldn't wait to bring you here. I couldn't think of a better restaurant for this special occasion."

James opened the door to the building, and Mara entered first. She felt a giddy anticipation as she looked at the chic, elegant surroundings, and a maitre d' with a winning smile showed them to a reserved corner table. After they were seated, a bottle of champagne was brought to the table.

"Champagne." Mara's eyes opened wide. "You know I don't really drink."

"But you must have a drink this evening, Mara. Please. For us?"

Mara looked deep into his eyes. There was more love there than she had ever seen.

"All right," Mara said as a waiter poured the bubbly liquid into two champagne flutes. Then he left them alone.

"Now." James held up his glass. "This is to us." He waited for Mara to lift her flute. Mara laughed when they clinked glasses.

"Okay, so this is to us. But what is this all about, James?"

James smiled with love. "I think you know."

*Mara looked down before she looked into his eyes
again.*

*"We've been together for two years," James continued.
"And I've never known a woman that I've loved more,
and that has made me feel so special. So loved." He
paused. "You are my perfect woman. You are the love of
my life, and I want to ask you, will you marry me, Mara?"
James leaned forward while their gazes remained locked.
Slowly, he touched his lips to hers then pressed them sweetly,
gently against Mara's trembling mouth. When the kiss
ended, tears welled up in Mara's eyes as James waited for
her answer. Finally she replied, "Yes, James. I will marry—"*

Buzz. The doorbell rang downstairs.

Mara sat up. "He's here already." She hurried
out of the room and down the stairs, wondering
how long she had been daydreaming. Quickly,
Mara looked through the peephole and opened
the door. "Hi. You got here so quick."

James stepped inside. "I wasn't very far away
when I called."

She kissed him on the cheek. "It won't take me
but a few minutes to get ready." Mara headed toward the stairs.

She entered her bedroom and caught a glimpse
of herself in the mirror. Mara was not happy with
what she saw. "You look a mess," she said to her reflection. Mara picked up her hairbrush, and with
several quick strokes smoothed her pulled-back
hairstyle. She added a dab of lipstick and put on
her eyeglasses. Mara looked in the mirror again.
"That's better," she said as she gave the hem of her
silky black T-shirt a couple of pulls, then dusted off
her black pants. Ready, Mara picked up her purse

and joined James in her living room. He was still standing at the front door.

"Why are you standing there like that? Maybe if you had come upstairs I wouldn't have felt so rushed."

"I didn't feel like it." He replied with a solemn face.

"Is there something wrong?"

James shrugged, then looked in her eyes. "Yeah, there is."

Mara squinted. "That guy's not giving you trouble at work again, is he?"

"No. No." James looked down. "It doesn't have anything to do with that. I'll tell you about it. Are you ready?" He placed his hand on the doorknob.

"Yeah, I'm ready. I wish you had given me a little more warning, though," Mara said. "When you called me, you really caught me off-guard."

"Oh." He looked at her. "Had you planned to work late?"

"No-o." Mara felt a little defensive. "It's just that you don't normally call me from work and in such a formal way, say," she dropped her voice, " 'I need to see you.' " She forced a laugh. "It sounded like this big deal." An image of James offering her an engagement ring flitted through her mind. "If I'd had more time, maybe I would have dressed for the occasion."

James tapped the doorknob with his finger tips. "What would you have done differently, Mara?"

The question was low and full of something Mara couldn't quite grasp. Whatever it was, it didn't feel good. "I don't know. Put on a skirt or something. I don't know. Should I have?" She tried to read his thoughts.

"It doesn't matter," James replied. "Let's go."

He opened the door and went outside. Mara locked it and they walked down the sidewalk to his car.

"Where are we going," she asked as James unlocked his car with a remote. They climbed inside.

James turned on the car. "To a new place I found."

"Oh, really?" Mara thought of her daydream. "Sounds exciting."

James stepped on the gas. "I think it is."

They drove in silence. The air was full of something that made Mara a little uneasy, but she didn't say anything to James about it. Finally, she heard herself ask, "Are you tired? You're more quiet than usual."

"No. I'm not tired, at least not from work."

His response increased her discomfort. Mara looked out the window and watched the houses and storefronts go by. *He's not tired from work. . . . That's a loaded answer if I ever heard one.*

But at the same time, Mara was uncertain if she was reading more into James's silence and words than what was meant. During their two years of being together, she had been accused, more than once, of thinking she could read his thoughts. And according to James, she was totally wrong. Over the last couple of months, Mara had made an effort to control her presumptiveness.

Chapter 2

A short time later they pulled up in front of Sammy's Bar and Grill.

"Is this the place?" Mara couldn't believe it.

"This is it," James replied.

There was nothing special about the exterior of the restaurant, and when they stepped inside, there was nothing special about the décor inside either. But the crowd was quite invigorating. There were lots of young, animated people, talking and enjoying happy hour. There were others seated at small tables having a bite to eat.

"Hey James, man. How you doin'?" a man seated on one of the barstools called.

"Can't complain." James smiled and raised his hand.

The exchange caught the attention of another happy hour patron. "James, what's goin' on?"

"Everything's the same, man," James replied as a waiter led them toward a table for two, seated them, then handed them menus.

Mara was more than a little surprised at the reception. "My goodness. You sure are popular here. You must come here quite often."

"I've been here a few times." James's eyes focused on the menu.

Mara looked at the people who were drinking and talking around the bar. The men were all sharp dressers, the kind that you would see in *GQ*. And some of the women were dressed in business attire as if they had come directly from work. But many of them were dressed in clothes that no office would allow. Mara turned her attention back to the menu. "Since you've been here so much," she couldn't hold back, "you have any recommendations?"

"I'd recommend the Famous n' Fancy hamburger. But of course you don't eat red meat any more."

"No, I don't." Her forehead creased. "But I haven't been eating red meat for over a year now. Is it a problem for you all of a sudden?"

"No. It's no problem for me. I think everybody should be able to make their own choices."

"So do I," Mara replied as their gazes locked.

James looked down again. "Well that's what I'm going to have, the Famous n' Fancy. Along with a beer."

Another waitress dressed in a white shirt and black skirt appeared at the side of their table. "Are you ready?" She looked at James.

"Are you?" James asked Mara.

"Yes, I'm ready," Mara replied. By now she was certain there was something very different about James's attitude toward her. "I'll take your tuna melt."

"What do you want that on? White? Wheat? Pumpernickel?"

"I'll take it on wheat," Mara replied.

"Okay." The waitress made some quick scratchy marks on her pad. "And you?"

"I'm going to do the Famous n' Fancy," James said. "And I want everything on it. And bring me a Bud."

"You've got it. You want anything to drink?' She looked at Mara again.

Mara looked at the menu. "Do you have lemonade?"

"Yeah, we do."

"Is it fresh squeezed," she asked, reluctantly.

"Mara," James said, intercepting the waitress's answer, "does this place look like it would have fresh-squeezed lemonade?"

She stared at him for just a second. "I'll take some iced tea," Mara said. "If you have it—sweetened."

"That we have," the waitress replied. "Be back with your drinks in just a minute. Sorry about the lemonade."

"No problem," Mara replied. When she looked back at James, he was eyeing one of the women who was standing and talking to a guy at the bar. It wasn't just a casual glance, mind you. He was really checking the woman out. Mara sat back and put both her hands on the table. "James, correct me if I'm wrong but . . . I feel like you're upset with me about something."

Slowly, he withdrew his gaze and looked at Mara. "Upset? No, I wouldn't say I'm upset." Then he looked down.

"You wouldn't say you're upset. Then what are you?"

"I'm just—uh, a little tired, Mara."

"Tired," she repeated as the waitress delivered the iced tea and beer.

"Yeah, I'm tired of this same old scene that we've been playing—day-after-day, week-after-week. We don't do anything exciting. You know." His brow creased. "Here we are in our early thirties and our lives are absolutely . . . boring."

Mara felt her mouth drop open. "I'm twenty-eight. And you've never said anything about this before."

"Well, I may not have said anything, but I surely tried to show you that—uh, I wanted a little bit more excitement."

"And when was that?" Mara sat forward as she tried to keep her voice down. She couldn't believe what James was saying.

"Think about it." He showed her his palm. "More than a few times I've asked you to go out and go dancing. And I wasn't talking about inter-pretive dance." James gave Mara a deadpan look. "I meant let's go to a club. I think you might have agreed once. But other than that you wanted to go to a movie, to an environmental rally, or you wanted to just go sit and talk at the coffee house. That's not my thing, Mara. Those are the things you want to do."

"But I met you at a coffee house, James. That's where we met. So of course, I would assume it was your thing. And when we first started talking, when we talked about the things that we liked and didn't like, you always said you didn't like going to clubs, that dancing was not something that appealed to you. And I told you that I didn't go out to clubs much. But it didn't mean I didn't like to dance." She stared at him. "And the truth is, I thought we had come to a place where we saw eye-to-eye when it came to these kinds of things."

"Well maybe that was good for then. But, uh, it's not for me anymore."

"Really?" Mara sat back.

"No, it's not." James looked away and shook his head.

"Well tell me." She glanced at the ceiling. "What is it that you want now? It sounds like you want to make some changes in this relationship. I guess that's what you're basically saying." Her heart beat faster.

"You could say that."

"I am saying it, James." Mara could feel her anger. "Look, don't play with me. We're too old to play. Say what you mean." Her voice went up and a couple of people turned around and looked at them.

James simply stared at her.

"Say something." She leaned forward. "Here you bring me to this place where people know you. I mean, you're this regular here in this bar that I knew nothing about. You've never invited me before. But now when you invite me you start telling me about what's wrong with our relationship."

"Here we are," the waitress said. "A tuna melt for you, and a Famous n' Fancy for you. Here's ketchup and hot sauce. Would you like anything else?"

Mara shook her head.

"This is cool," James replied before the waitress walked away.

James studied his sandwich, while Mara cut her tuna melt in half as she waited for an answer.

"The truth is," James began, "I don't think that we can make the kind of changes that I'm looking for, Mara."

A tremor went through her. "What do you mean we can't make the kind of changes you're looking for? Tell me what you're thinking. If you don't talk to me, how can you make that kind of decision?"

"Because I know you, Mara. I know you. And the woman that I've come to know over these two years is, uh, you know, she's a wonderful woman. She's kind. She's smart. Gonna get ahead in life. All those things. But, uh, the other things, Mara, are just not you."

Mara held half of the sandwich near her mouth, then she put it down. "What isn't me, James?"

"I mean, going out to clubs, and dressing sexy and, you know, flirting." He licked his lips. "You know what I mean."

"Oh, I see." She looked at the woman James had been checking out. "So it isn't that the relationship or what we do isn't exciting enough. Basically, you're telling me, I'm not exciting enough."

He gave a small shrug. Silence followed.

"James!" There was a plea in Mara's voice.

He looked into her eyes.

"Is that what you're telling me?"

James looked at his burger and took a bite. He chewed a bit before he answered. "Look Mara, I don't want to hurt you. It isn't about putting the blame anywhere. We are who we are. And, uh, and sometimes time reveals things you may not have noticed in the beginning."

"And what time has shown you is, I'm simply not

exciting enough. I'm not sexy enough for you anymore. You want a woman like the one standing up
there at that counter showing the world everything she's got." Her anger spilled over.

"I'm saying that she looks pretty good to me,"
James replied.

Mara's heart dropped, and suddenly she knew if
she ate even one bite of the tuna melt she would
choke on it. Her boyfriend of two years had just
told her that she wasn't sexy enough for him. She
wasn't appealing anymore.

The waitress reappeared at the table. "Are you
okay over here? Is there anything else I can get
you?"

James replied, "No. We're fine."

But Mara said, "You can box this up for me."
She lifted her entire plate. "I'm going to take it
with me."

"What's wrong," the waitress inquired.

"Nothing's wrong with the food," Mara replied.
"I just need to go. So if you can box it up for me,
please." Mara handed the waitress the plate. "I'd
really appreciate it."

"Whatever you want," the waitress replied before she walked away.

"Now look at you. What did you do that for?"
James asked. "You're making a scene."

Mara struggled to keep her voice down. "I am
trying not to make a scene, James Coldwater. But
I'm not going to sit here and eat with you after
we've been together for two years and you can just
sit and tell me what I'm not. That I don't excite
you any more. That basically, I'm boring. And that
you want more, but you don't think I'm capable of
that. I'm just not going to sit here and have a meal

with you like this, when you've had plenty of opportunities, if you cared for me, to really share your feelings with me before it got to this." Her eyes narrowed. "If you just wanted to step out and experience—" Her head motioned toward the woman at the bar. Mara paused as she looked James dead in the eyes. "I think that's what this is really about. As a matter of fact, I think you've already done it, because this conversation feels like it's after the fact. And since it is, I'm through with you, James. I am done."

The waitress returned with Mara's box.

Mara stood up and put her purse on her shoulder. She looked down at James. "I hope you find the excitement you're looking for."

"Thank you." Mara took the food from the waitress and walked out the door.

As Mara walked down the street she felt as if her heart were in her hand. As soon as she could, Mara disappeared into one of the stores that was part of the strip mall, and, with her insides like jelly, she used her cell phone to call a taxi.

Chapter 3

"There's my car, right there," Sharon said, pointing her vehicle out to Mara. "But why don't you go with me to the dance studio and register with me?"

"I'm not going anywhere with this hat on my head," Mara replied.

"What do mean, you're not going anywhere?" Sharon leaned back and studied Mara's hat. "You've already been to the coffee shop, so what difference is it going to make if you go and check out the samba classes?"

Mara glanced at her. "Look, don't give me a hard time." She turned the corner. "I'm going to go home. I need to wash my hair. Then I have to blow-dry it. I need a hot-oil treatment too."

"I don't know why you put yourself through all that trouble." Sharon ran her fingers through her hair. "I've already told you if you're not going to lock your hair, you should wear some other natural style. Just wash it and let it dry naturally." She turned and faced Mara. "You could do that with your hair."

"You don't know my hair," Mara retorted.

"Then wash it and braid it and let it dry," Sharon replied. "Your hair is beautiful; you don't need all that heat on it."

Mara's chin stuck out stubbornly. "It's my hair, and I'll do what I want."

"All right. You're right. I'm done with the hair thing," Sharon replied. "I'm just trying to help you turn a new leaf or something. Ever since you and James broke up, you haven't been doing a dog-gone thing. Nothing. Do you hear me? That's why I'm inviting you to take the samba classes. It'll do you good."

"I don't want to hear it," Mara said.

Sharon made a face. "I'm sure I don't have to tell you how badly you've been moping around. So, you know. At least if you take these classes, it will give you something to look forward to."

"I don't know anything about samba," Mara replied, but a wistful look crossed her face.

"Well that's what classes are for," Sharon threw back. "You go and you learn."

Sharon's insistence pushed Mara's buttons. "And the truth is, how many sisters have you seen taking samba classes?"

"I–I," Sharon stumbled. "Not many."

"You haven't seen one. Have you?"

"No." Sharon looked down. "But when you think about the samba and Brazil, there are all kinds of sisters there dancing . . . darker than you could ever be. So don't pull the sister thing on me because I'm Puerto Rican." Sharon stuck out her bottom lip. "The samba is beautiful and sexy, Mara. You'd feel so good doing it, if you'd only try."

"I'd definitely shake up James if I did. I can't believe he made that crack about my interpretive dance classes."

Sharon rolled her eyes. "Don't bring James up again. Plu-eze. Let him stay where he is, back there where you two broke up. What was that, about a month ago?" Sharon shook her head. "He wasn't right for you anyway."

"What?" Mara pulled over and stopped the car. "This is my first time hearing this."

"Well." Sharon scratched her neck. "Mara, you know, I have never been a big fan of James's. I never talked about it while you were with him, but that wasn't what I was supposed to do. So I'm telling you now, he wasn't the right one. He was not the one." She looked out the window. "Always trying to act all innocent and everything. He was always looking at other women. Every opportunity he got." She looked straight ahead, and her nose lifted like she smelled something. "He was just sneaky with it, and I couldn't stand him."

"Uh! I can't believe you're saying this."

"Well I am," Sharon replied. "But that's all I'm going to say about that. So what are you going to do, Mara? Come on now. Drive me to the studio. It's just about four blocks away. Then you can drop me back over here at my car."

Mara looked undecided. "How long will the classes last, Sharon?" Before Sharon could answer, Mara continued. "And see, you won't even be in my class. I'll be just starting off."

"What difference will it make if I'm not in your class? You'll have fun. You'll have fun no matter who is there." Sharon's eyes brightened. "We'll still be able to go at the same time because it's a large dance studio, and they have more than one instructor. We could have such fun. Come on, Mara."

"I asked you how long the classes will last."

"I don't know." Sharon threw up her hands. "Drive me over there and find out for yourself. It won't take but a second."

"All right. I'll see." She placed both hands on the steering wheel. "I do need to do something. And I've got a confession."

"What?"

"I've always seen samba dancers and thought, boy, I'd love to move and dance like that. So I'd try it in secret."

"Why in secret?"

"Because." Mara looked down. "It really wasn't my style."

Sharon made another face. "If you like it, it is your style. No. It wasn't who people thought you were. See, you've been a people pleaser for too long. It is way past time for you to get out of that. And this is your opportunity."

Mara pulled back out into the street, and under Sharon's guidance she drove around the corner and down a few blocks.

"This is it, right here." Sharon pointed to JC's Dance Studio. "Whoa. Check out the big, fancy stretch limousine out front. I wonder who's riding in that."

Mara glanced at the vehicle before she parked. "There's no telling."

They got out of the car and crossed the street.

Just as Mara and Sharon were entering the building, the front door opened. A tall, striking man with skin the color of burnished honey and jet-black hair stepped outside. A shorter man with a lithe physique that he displayed under a muscle shirt was behind him. The shorter man said, "You know, if you hadn't stopped by, you were going to be in trouble." He slapped the taller man's forearm. "How long are you going to be in town?"

"I'm flying back later on tonight."

"That's a shame. We could have had dinner or something if you had given me some notice."

"Yes, that would have been nice. But I come here, and sometimes my schedule is so full," the taller man replied as he glanced at Mara and then Sharon.

"May I help you ladies?" the shorter man asked.

"Yes," Sharon replied. "We're thinking about taking samba lessons."

"Great." He rubbed his hands together. "New classes will be starting in about two weeks." He pointed toward the interior of the building. "Inside there is a table with all kinds of information on it. As soon as you reach the end of this hallway it's going to be to your left. We've got brochures for the beginning, intermediate, and advanced classes available." His smile was genuine. "So pick up whatever interests you and I'll be in shortly to talk to you about it."

Both men stepped to the side. Mara glanced at the taller one, who smelled like the most expensive men's cologne. Her gaze drifted from his smooth, plum-colored T-shirt to his black pants that looked as if they were made from the finest of fabrics. He flashed Mara and Sharon a beguiling smile.

Mara smiled, but she tried to hide how much she was aware of his good looks underneath the loopy brim of her hat. Hiding impaired her vision, and Mara tripped on the lip of concrete just outside the door. The tall man's arms were around her before she hit the ground and made an even bigger fool of herself. For just a moment their bodies pressed together while Mara's face rested against his chest. She couldn't help but be aware of how ultrahard and muscular his body was, and how his shirt was even softer than it appeared.

"Be careful," he warned.

"Thank you," Mara replied as he released her. She stood up and straightened her hat that by now, Mara was certain, made her look like a female Jed Clampett from the old *Beverly Hillbillies* sitcom. She hurried up the hall behind Sharon, toward a table of pamphlets, posters, and flyers.

"Did you see him?" Sharon picked up the flyer for the intermediate class. "My God! I didn't know they made them like that. Somebody must have cut him out of a magazine and brought him to life. The short one wasn't too bad either."

Mara sighed. "Yeah, he was amazing, wasn't he?"

Sharon put her hand on her hip. "Amazing . . . He was certainly that. Enough to knock you down." She smiled. "But he's out of our league. I think he's the one who's riding around in that limousine."

"Yeah, he looked like the type that would use a limousine as daily transportation." Mara peered up the hall before she picked up a beginner's sheet. Sharon looked up when the door closed and the shorter man approached them with his hand outstretched, inviting a handshake.

"Okay. Now I can give you all of my attention. You caught me talking to the man that the studios are named after."

"Really?" Mara's eyes brightened. She looked at Sharon.

"Absolutely. That was JC." He made quote signs with his fingers. "And I'm Roberto. I own this studio. And you are?"

Sharon took his hand. "I'm Sharon Vegas."

"And I'm Mara Scott."

"Great to meet you ladies. And you're thinking about taking some classes." He motioned toward the table.

"I definitely am," Sharon said.

"And what about you?" he addressed Mara.

"Maybe." She closed one eye.

"Why maybe? I see you picked up one of the beginner's flyers. And as you can see, we're running a special. Six weeks of lessons at eight dollars a session. Normally that would cost you sixty dollars, but with the special, it's forty-eight dollars. And if you have any kind of dancing bones in you, by the end of those six weeks, I'll guarantee that you'll be samba-ing with the best of them."

Mara laughed lightly.

Roberto nodded. "You see. That's what this is about. It's about having fun. It's about showing who you are."

Mara laughed again. "I can believe that."

Roberto touched her arm. "So you must come. I'm personally going to be looking for you on June fifth, when the class starts. Okay?"

"Are you going to be the instructor?" Mara asked.

"No. Normally I don't teach the beginner's classes,

or the intermediate. But I'll be around to encourage you." He crossed his heart. "I promise. At least for the first two lessons."

"Okay. It's a deal," Mara said. "If I see you during my first two lessons I'll continue to come."

"The bet is on," Roberto replied.

"So what do we wear?" Mara asked.

"Whatever you want to wear. But I suggest that you wear something that you can really move in. Something like a flared short skirt that would show how your hips are moving." His smile broadened. "That's always encouraging. And some shoes with little sturdy heels. Once you decide that you really like it, then I'll turn you on to some of the professional footwear and clothing. But in the beginning, we just want to get your feet wet."

"Okay," Mara replied.

"And you too, since you're going to take the intermediate class." He smiled at Sharon.

"Yeah, I've already got some stuff," she said. "And I can't wait to put it on. They're wild, Mara. I'll lend you some."

"I don't know about that." Mara looked skeptical.

"I like that." Roberto's eyes twinkled. "I don't need to encourage her. I think if I did, she'd be too much for any of us to handle."

Sharon stuck out her tongue and shook her hips. "I can't wait."

"I'll see both of you on June fifth." Roberto shook his index finger. "And don't forget our bet." He looked at Mara.

"Don't you forget," she said as she and Sharon walked toward the door.

"I think this is going to be fun," Mara exclaimed

as they dashed across the street, then jumped into her car.

"I told you so." Sharon shimmied her shoulders.

Mara smiled. "And if any of the men taking lessons look like JC," she made quote signs with her fingers, "it will be fun in more ways than I ever imagined."

"See there." Sharon snapped her fingers. "Things are looking up already. James, eat your heart out."

Chapter 4

Mara threw her head back and moved her hips as her feet shuffled to the samba beat. She had never felt so alive, so beautiful, in her life, and Mara enjoyed every gesture as her classmates clapped and shouted their approval. At the end of the music and her performance, there was a burst of applause as Mara bowed dramatically and laughed as she attempted to catch her breath. She continued to smile as she walked from the middle of the studio floor to join her colleagues on the sidelines.

"Woman!" Roberto exclaimed. "I knew I did the right thing when I told you to start going to the intermediate class. What made you think you were supposed to be in the beginner's class in the first place? When you started to dance, it was like a goddess had come alive on the dance floor. I can imagine what you will look like when we get you to jazz up your style a bit. You know, some wild hair. More makeup."

Mara shook her head. "Stop, Roberto. Stop. I can't take all this praise."

"Take it, baby. Take it," he said. "You deserve it."

"You do!" Sharon beamed. "Mara! You've been holding back on us." She put both hands on her hips. "How can you do this to me? Here I am thinking I'm the intermediate dancer and you come along, get in my class, and outdo me. But I'm glad you did." She tilted her chin down. "And now I see you and I'm like, who-oa, is she an intermediate dancer or is she a professional?"

Mara covered her face. "Both of you, don't do this. I'm beginning to feel shy."

"Well, you weren't shy out there on that floor," Sharon retorted.

Another dancer came up and touched Mara's shoulder. "You are great, girl. It looks like the samba is in your blood."

"Thanks," Mara replied, then looked at Sharon. "All I can say is I love it. Absolutely love it."

"I'm glad you do," Roberto said. "Because guess what?"

"What?" Mara dabbed at the perspiration that beaded her brow.

"I want you to enter the state competition."

"What?" Mara's eyes widened.

"Ye-es," Roberto said.

"Oh no, I can't do that," Mara replied.

"What do you mean you can't do that? I'm telling you I want you to." He held her chin. "This is a personal invitation. If I say that you should enter, then that means that I know you have a chance."

"Roberto, I've only been taking samba classes for two months."

"It looks like you've been taking them for years," he replied.

"She was taking it for years," Sharon interjected. "She was a closet samba dancer. She was around here doing interpretive dance," she turned in a circle with her hands over her head "and then she'd go in her room and practice the samba."

"That was supposed to be a secret, Sharon."

"You shouldn't dance so well. It's obvious you didn't just start."

Roberto got in Mara's face again. "I don't know what you did in the past, what kind of closet you were in, but you have the makings of someone who could win. When you start to dance, you have the attitude and all. So I want you to enter the competition, Mara."

"With all those people who have been dancing for years?" She looked unconvinced.

"There is the advanced competition and there is the intermediate. And truth be told, I think you could compete in the advanced, but because you are taking intermediate classes, you should enter the single female competition in that division. But whatever you do, compete, please."

Mara looked around at the other dancers. "It's one thing to come in here and get comfortable with everybody and dance, but it's another thing to be watched and judged." She shook her head. "It's something I don't want to do, Roberto."

"Do we have to convince you to do everything?" He looked away with disgust. "I tell you what. Do not give me an answer today. There are a few more days to enter, so I want you to think about it, Mara." His face turned serious. "Think about it. You're good. You have the makings of a beautiful samba dancer. Why wouldn't you?" He looked deep into her eyes. "Don't let your fears stop you from being all that you can be."

Mara started to interrupt.

"That's all I'm going to say." Roberto ended his plea. He touched her arm. "Good job, Mara." And walked away.

Mara and Sharon put their towels and other dance essentials into their bags and walked toward the door. They were silent as they stepped outside the building.

"Mara," Sharon began. "I think you should think about this."

"I know that's how you feel. But I just . . . you know, everybody's not the kind of person who wants to be out front and judged." She shook her head. "I just don't like the thought of somebody judging me."

"People judge you every day. Anytime you walk outside your door and someone looks at you, they come up with some kind of thoughts about you. You need to let that feeling go."

Mara's lips pressed together. "See, for someone like you, it's easy. You're extroverted, you're outgoing, and you've always been. Things roll off of you so easily, no matter what it is. And I take things so much to heart. I really do. I always have."

"I know you're sensitive. I understand that. But look, maybe you need to learn to use that to your advantage. Whatever they say, if it hurts you or not, just take it. I look at it and say 'They don't know who I am. And I am going to prove to them that I am more than they ever imagined.' That's what I say." Sharon waved her thumb in front of her chest.

"And that's one of the things I love about you."

Mara put her arm around Sharon's shoulder. "And that's why you should enter the contest. Enter in my place."

"Roberto didn't ask me. No matter how I wish he had." Sharon gave her a doe-eyed look. "He didn't. He asked you, and you need to think about that."

Mara paused. "I will."

Sharon nodded. "All right. I'll see you tomorrow."

"Bye," Mara replied before she walked to her car.

As Mara drove home she thought about the dance routine she had choreographed and the reactions of Roberto and her classmates. It felt good to be applauded, to be seen in such a light. When Mara got home, her father greeted her at the door.

"Hey, Dad. How you doin'?"

"I'm makin' it," he replied in his familiar downtrodden manner.

"Well I've got some good news for you."

"What's that?"

"I've been asked to compete in a state samba contest."

"Samba?"

"Yeah, samba, Dad. You know, the dance that you see those Brazilian women doing that catches everybody's eye, including yours, I'm sure."

"Jumping Jehoshaphat. When did you start doing that kind of dancing?" He looked truly shocked.

"Oh, a couple of months ago."

"I thought you liked that interpretive dance."

"I do." Mara picked at her sleeve. "But we all

need to find some new interests in life. And that is an outright hint, if you are wondering about it."

"Change is for you younger folks, Mara." Nathan Scott replied. "I don't know nothing about change. I don't have the energy for it."

"Well, Dad, if you're going to remain here among the living, you've got to think about change, or at least do the old things with some enthusiasm. You always sound so drained."

"That's because that's how I feel." He paused. "Since your mother died I just don't have the willpower I used to have."

"Dad, Mom died over two years ago, and I think Mom would want you to . . . she knows you loved her and that you've grieved for her, but now you've got to go at life differently than what you're doing." *Now I sound like Sharon.*

"It's easier said than done, Mara."

"I know. I miss Mom too." She patted his arm. "But I understand that you and I are still here, and we've got to go on."

"Well, I don't want to talk about it anymore. Not right now. But I guess I should congratulate you on being asked to enter that contest, even though it's quite a leap from interpretive dance to shaking your body in front of folks like that." He looked at her from beneath bushy, disapproving brows.

Can he not go along with me just once without some kind of judgmental comment? "Oh, Dad." Mara replied.

Later she removed some leftover pasta from the refrigerator and warmed it in the microwave. Mara read a book as she ate, then took a bath and went to bed.

The following morning Mara went to the gym,

not so much for the exercise, but for the spalike facilities. An hour later she emerged from the whirlpool, wrapped in a towel. Mara walked slowly, reliving the pummeling waters that had stimulated her body, and forced her stubborn muscles to relax. She felt as limp as a rag when she opened the door to the steam sauna. The burst of hot, moist air gave her a pleasant welcome. As she closed the door behind her, a white manufactured cloud scented with eucalyptus embraced her. Mara secured her towel and took a seat on one of the lower benches. Her eyes narrowed to protect themselves from the steam. Relaxed, she glanced around the room.

There were three men sitting in various poses. Mara could have secretly indulged herself by studying their chiseled, smooth chests and their muscles that rippled whenever they moved, but instead she closed her eyes and listened to their conversations, for what good would lust do when there was no one in her life that she could vent it on?

Two of the men were deep into verbal volleyball. There seemed to be no room in either of their minds for compromise. It was their way or no way. It made Mara think of the Brazilian project. *I bet that's exactly how that land developer that owns the site that we're working on thinks. Jairo Camara.* She shook her head. *No matter what information we give and how we've tried to open his eyes to make this project unique, he just can't see it. At least that's what we are being told. He's a total blockhead. Why can't he see that integrating the natural landscape into the design would make it that much more powerful? And beautiful.* She leaned her head back. *I don't understand a man with as much money as this guy is supposed to have not having some vision. It's like he wants to destroy those trees just to destroy them. He's gone along with everything else, but he is hellbent on getting rid of those old, indigenous trees. Well, I don't care what the others have decided. I'm not going to give in. Somehow I've got to make him see that we need to preserve land like this. There's enough concrete and asbestos in this world. That's what killed Mama. Asbestos. Manmade materials like that are hurting us, and if we just make an effort to balance our creations with nature, our lives would be much healthier and richer.* Mara licked her lips that tingled from the eucalyptus. *Plus I promised Mama, after she died, that every chance I got I'd fight for the environment, and I'm going to do just that. Mr. Camara himself might be at the big meeting next week, and I'm going to present my case no matter what.*

Chapter 5

Mara took a shower after the sauna, tightened her hair on top of her head in a curly, unruly puff, and donned a baggy pair of pants and an oversized top before she put on her glasses. She felt wonderful as she headed out of the building. It was a beautiful day and she looked at the clouds as she walked toward the parking lot. She stopped at the curb to let an approaching car pass. Her nerves went from calm to spiked when she recognized James's Grand Am, and there he was, with a woman beside him.

Just keep going. Keep going, Mara said to herself, but he stopped right in front of her.

"How you doin'?" He smiled out the window.

Mara rested on one hip and crossed her arms. "I'm fine." She didn't want to ask how he was but she did. "And you?"

"I'm doin' great. Just great. Thought I'd come to the gym and work out a little. And this is a friend of mine." He motioned toward the woman beside him, "who has never been here before, so I brought her along."

The woman placed her hand on his thigh and leaned on James as she strained to see Mara through his open window. "Hi." Her deep cut top allowed Mara to see more than she was interested in seeing.

"Hello," Mara replied.

The woman disappeared from Mara's view.

"So everything's good for you?" James rephrased his earlier question.

What do you want me to say? That I miss you and you've got that woman in the car? Not in a million years. "Things are really good for me," Mara replied. "As a matter of fact I've been asked to enter a state samba dance competition." *Is that sexy enough for you?*

James's brows knitted. "Samba competition?"

"You didn't know I danced the samba, did you?" Mara donned a superior look.

"No. I don't think I've ever heard you mention it before."

"Really?" She smiled coyly. "It's funny how you can be around someone for years and some things just never come up." Mara paused. "So yeah, the owner of one of the local studios asked me to enter."

"For some reason I just can't see you doing the samba, Mara," James smirked.

"Oh-h, I love the dance. It's so-o sensuous and sexy. And so I'm going to enter."

"Swear to God?" James looked truly shocked.

"Absolutely," Mara replied.

"And where is this competition going to be?"

Now it was Mara's turn to be surprised. "I'm not certain, but I think it's going to be here in Orlando."

"Really?" Once again James's brow furrowed. "I think I'd like to come. When is it?"

Mara's stomach tightened "He just asked me, so I don't know the date right off of the top of my head, but it's coming up really soon. I'm sure you'll be able to find the information on the Internet." Mara was determined not to help James or invite him.

"I'll get one of those artsy community newspapers. They have all the local events. I'm sure it will be in there."

"I'm sure it will." Mara remained falsely cheery. "But I've got to go now. I've got things to do."

"All right." James looked her up and down. "I'll see you around."

Mara did not reply. She walked away from his car and hoped her body language said she could care less if she saw him or not. Mara got to her car, climbed inside, and sat there with the windows rolled up.

"Why? Why did it have to happen that way? Why did I have to see him when I was looking like this? Doggone it. I'm so mad I could just . . . spit." Mara raged. "And he was so cool." She made a face. "And I can tell he thought he had something sitting beside him. That hootchie mama. Well, they deserve each other." She leaned her head against the headrest and closed her eyes. "But I wish they hadn't seen me like this."

Mara saw herself come out of the fitness center. In her vision she wore a purple fitted exercise set that clung to breasts and hips she didn't have in real life. There was just enough cleavage, and her belly was as flat as a board. Mara took the ends of the fluffy towel that rested around her neck and patted her temples as she walked with confidence toward the parking lot.

"What's up? Leaving so soon?" *a deep voice asked.*

"We hope not," *another added.*

Mara turned and saw two good-looking men with perfect physiques smiling at her.

"Yes. I'm leaving." *She smiled enticingly.* "I'm so tired."

"Don't be tired," *the taller one replied.* "Come back in and sit in the sauna with us. Maybe we can enjoy the hot tub together."

"I've done that already," *Mara replied.*

"Aw-w baby," *the shorter man said.* "Isn't there anything we can do to get you to spend a little time with us?"

She waited for a car to pass. "Not today." *Mara smiled as the car stopped in front of her.*

"Hey, Mara."

"Well, hello, James," *she said, surprised.*

"How are you?"

"I'm fine," *Mara replied.*

James looked at the two men who were standing at the entrance to the center. They were still checking her out.

"Aren't you going to introduce me, James?" *Mara saw knees full of cellulite sticking out from an embarrassingly short skirt.*

"Hey." *A voice interrupted.*

Mara turned.

"Don't hesitate to come back in and find us if you change your mind," *the taller man said.*

She smiled.

"Why don't you just go inside and mind your own business," *James retorted.*

Mara waved and the men entered the building. Serene, she looked at James again. "I said, aren't you going to introduce me?"

He hesitated. "Sure. Adrian this is Mara. Mara, Adrian."

Adrian leaned onto James's thigh. "Hello."

Mara had to fight not to laugh. Adrian wore heavy blue eye shadow that weighed her eyelids down, and a white lipstick that caused her lips to look like two frosted Twinkies. But worst of all, Mara could see from the loose tracks in the top of her head her weave was in bad need of repair. "Hello," she replied, then said, "Well, I've got to go now." She watched James look at her with unbridled desire.

"Maybe I can call you later," he said desperately.

"Not in a million years," Mara replied.

She could feel his eyes on her as she walked to her car.

"Yes. Yes." Mara opened her eyes. "That's how I want him to feel. I want James to feel that he missed out when he let me go." She looked in the rearview mirror. "And I am going to do it one way or another." She swiped at the hot tear that trickled down the side of her nose. "I am sick of living out my life in daydreams. Why can't things be the way I want them to be?" Mara swallowed hard. "Well, I am not going to sit by and just cry about it. Out of everything my mother gave me, she helped me believe I could make whatever I wanted out of my life, and I'll be damned if I'll prove her wrong. I've got the career. Now I want an exciting, fulfilling personal life. And I intend to get it."

Chapter 6

Mara went back into the gymnasium. She saw Sharon talking to one of Roberto's students. She walked up and stood beside them in silence.

"Hey!" Sharon said.

"Hey," Mara replied. "Well, what do you think?" Mara extended her arms and showed off the short, flouncy skirt that rested below her navel. Above it was a matching midriff top. Mara swirled, and the bright purple, orange, and blue material rippled.

"And you even found some purple shoes that match it exactly." Sharon made a circle with her thumb and index finger.

"Thank you," Mara said.

"But I've got a question for you." Sharon leaned close to Mara's face.

"What?" Mara said skeptically.

"Where is the makeup that I gave you?"

"I've got on makeup," Mara replied.

"You've got on the kind of makeup that you'd wear to the office, which is hardly any at all."

"So. . . . Makeup is makeup," Mara retorted.

"No, it's not." Sharon put her hand on her hip. "Where is that makeup I gave you? I gave you that kohl to make your eyes stand out."

"It's in my purse."

"Good. You've got to have dark eyes, Mara. You don't want to look dead out there. You've got all these bright colors on, and your face looks totally dead. At least you took my advice about wearing contacts. And you've got some blush, right?"

"Can't you see it?" Mara was a little perturbed.

Sharon rolled her eyes. "Don't spare the kohl, hype up the blush, and use more lipstick. Put some pressure on that tube. I can see you tried a little bit." Sharon focused on Mara's mouth. "But let me see bright purple. I want to see your lips from over there in the stands."

"Sharon, I—"

"Go." Sharon gave her a gentle shove. "Before anybody sees you. And make your hair fuller. Make it wild. Give us the wild-child look."

"I'll try." Mara headed toward the ladies' room.

She was glad there was no one there when she stepped inside. Mara leaned toward the mirror. "I can see the makeup. Why can't Sharon see it?" She bit her lip. "But I guess if Sharon can't see it while she's standing close to me, the judges won't be able to see a thing. All right." Mara made up her mind. She removed the kohl, blush, and lipstick from her purse. "Sharon wants dark eyes, I'll give her dark eyes." She traced her eyes in an elaborate fashion, including small wings at the tips. The result was a dramatic wide-eyed look. "Holy cow!" Mara laughed. "But now I need more eyebrows." She searched inside her purse for an eyebrow pencil. After she found it, she created more brows. "All right. Now some blush." She went at it heavier than she'd ever applied it. At the end she smoothed some of it in with her fingertips. Lastly, Mara applied the lipstick with deep strokes, shaping her lips fully. When she was done, she looked at herself, and said with awe and laughter, "Who is this woman?" Mara answered her own question. "It's a wild woman." Next, she pulled at her hair and fluffed out the tight corkscrews until the style was fuller and wider. The transformation was amazing.

"Now maybe those large, dangly earrings that I bought yesterday will work." Mara had tried the earrings on before she left home, but felt they were too much. She pulled the earrings out of her purse and put them on. They dangled sassily.

Mara stared at the image that looked back. It was unbelievable. "I don't even recognize myself," she proclaimed to her reflection as a surge of nervous energy coursed through her. "I can't get more ready than this." She was pleased with the results, and grinned like a teenager as she opened the bathroom door.

There were many more people in the gymnasium when Mara emerged, and this time it took a little effort to spot Sharon. Mara walked over to her and tapped her on the shoulder. Sharon turned around. Her expression said it all.

"Look at you! I knew that the makeup would make a difference, but I didn't know it would make this big of a difference. Oh my God, you are beautiful."

"You can say that again," the male dancer who had been talking to Sharon echoed.

"And I feel it." Mara smiled. "So no matter what

happens in this gymnasium, tonight I feel like I've broken through some kind of a barrier. I feel like a brand-new woman." She lifted her chin.

"That's the spirit," Sharon said with admiration in her eyes. "Did you get a number? A number that tells where you are in the line-up?"

"I've got it right here," Mara replied. "I'm next to the last person to compete in my group."

"Then they'll have the advanced competition," Sharon informed her.

"Yes." Mara took a deep breath.

"So how are you feeling?" Sharon inquired.

"I feel good," Mara replied. "And I'm ready."

"Great." Sharon touched her arm. "You just go out there and show them your stuff. And like you said, no matter what happens, the way you look . . . you're a winner tonight."

Mara's smile broadened. "Thanks."

By the time the competition got under way, the gymnasium bleachers were half full of spectators. The competitors sat on the bleachers nearest to the floor. There was a special section of chairs near the entrance for the VIP, while a table of judges stretched out across the back doors, which were locked.

The competition was in full swing when Mara thought about James's remark about attending the contest. Her eyes searched the crowd, but she did not see him. Afterwards, Mara settled into watching the couples in the intermediate competition compete. Her adrenaline rose as the singles competition began. Mara's confidence increased as she watched some of the performances and dimmed while watching others.

"Mara." Sharon leaned over her shoulder from the bleacher above. "Isn't that the guy whom the studio is named for? You know, the good-looking guy that we saw the first time we came here?"

"Where?" Mara asked, but she continued to focus on the competition.

"He's walking in here now with that bodyguard type behind him."

Mara looked in the direction in which Sharon pointed, and there was no doubt in her mind that it was the same man. She watched him walk with a kind of masculine authority that was powerful yet graceful. Mara got the feeling as she watched him that he was accustomed to giving orders to people following his commands.

On anyone else his vermillion shirt and olive-green pants might have been borderline gaudy, but their vibrancy simply matched his persona. Mara and Sharon watched him go over to Roberto, who stood up to greet him, before Roberto walked him over to a special seat in the VIP section.

Reluctantly, Mara turned her attention to the gymnasium floor. Two more competitors performed their routines before it was Mara's turn.

"All right now." Sharon patted her on the shoulder. "You give these people everything you've got. You hear?"

Mara nodded determinedly before she walked over to the judges and gave them her number. Minutes later she walked to the middle of the gymnasium floor and she struck her beginning pose. But when the music began Mara froze. She looked at the hundreds of faces that stared at her. *I can't pay attention to them. I've got to focus on the music. If I don't, I'm not going to be able to do it.* For a moment, Mara saw JC's face. There was intensity there. Extreme intensity.

"You can do whatever you set your mind to, Mara." She heard her mother's voice inside her head. *I can. Can't I? I can, and I can do this.* She bolstered her confidence. *What do I have to lose?*

Mara felt an inner burst of energy that synchronized with the music. It was as if that energy made Mara and the music one. She danced her feelings through her arms, her facial expressions, through the toss of her head and the powerful movement of her hips. Mara combined her knowledge of fluid movement from interpretive dance with the dramatic moves of the samba.

When the last drumbeat sounded, Mara was in full motion; her entire body reflected the beat as she flung her hips, and her hands out and in, then up over her head. Applause filled the gymnasium, and Mara felt her hands come up to her lips in a position of prayer, before tears came to her eyes. She returned to her seat. Sharon gave her a huge hug from behind.

"Oh my God, you were the best. You were the best," Sharon repeated.

Mara reveled in Sharon's praise as she was shown several thumbs-up and the competition continued. By the time it was over Mara felt somewhat overwhelmed by the world of samba; the colors, the people and the personalities flared on the gymnasium floor as well as around her. It was a world that she knew little about. In this world there was no restraint. Emotions were expressed fully, from anger to love to praise to censure. Mara wasn't sure she actually belonged here, but for this one evening, Mara was glad she had come and made her presence known.

They all waited as the judges turned in their votes and the numbers were tallied. It wasn't long before the announcer began to name the winners. Mara held her breath as the winners in various categories were called.

"And the winner," the announcer began, "in the single female category, in the intermediate competition is . . . Mara Scott."

Mara and Sharon jumped to their feet. They hugged each other, and before Mara knew it she was across the floor, accepting her trophy. She looked at it before she clutched it tightly against her breasts. Mara smiled at the crowd as her heart beat wildly. It was an exhilarating moment. She remained, along with the other winners, on the floor until the winners in the advanced category were announced.

"Now for the big announcement." The announcer raised his hand as he surveyed the gymnasium. "There's going to be a national contest. And all the names of the winners here," he pointed toward the group that included Mara, "along with other winners from various states, will be put into a drawing. Four names, representing the four regions of the country, will be drawn! Those lucky contestants will win a two-week vacation for two, in Rio de Janeiro!"

Everyone applauded along with yelps and yells. Then, as if on cue, a wonderful samba tune began to play. The winners, and anyone else who was willing, began a vivacious samba explosion on the floor. For a moment, Mara stood in the midst of the mayhem as she searched for Sharon. Mara was surprised to see James approaching her with out-stretched arms.

"I would not have believed it in a thousand years." He smiled. "If you had paid me, I would not have believed it."

Mara looked at him. "Well, shame on you. What do you mean you wouldn't have believed it even if some one had paid you?"

"I mean—I just . . . look at you. Mm-mm-mm. You are gorgeous. You never looked this way when you were with me."

Mara crossed her arms. "And so what does that say about you?"

James chuckled and his eyes burned bright. "Well, can I get a hug or something?" He continued to hold his arms out.

Mara was about to reply when she felt someone touch her shoulder. She looked up. It was the man.

"He wants a hug. All I want is a dance," he said.

Mara couldn't believe it. *Why does he want to dance with me?* But still, the answer came quick. It was a no-brainer. "I'd love to dance."

Immediately, JC pulled her toward him and started to samba. Out of the corner of her eye, Mara saw James stick his hands in his pockets.

"I'm glad you won." He smiled down at her. "In my mind, there was no one in your division that came close to you."

"Thank you," Mara replied.

JC controlled their dance effortlessly, and Mara was aware of a couple of photographers who were taking photos. "By the way," JC asked, "why did you choose that song to dance to?"

Still baffled because JC had asked her to dance, Mara told the simple truth. "I fell in love with it the first time I heard it. It moved something inside of me. It's almost difficult to explain."

He studied her face. "I think I understand. That song seems to hold a special power for some people."

Mara had danced a few times with some of her male classmates, but it was nothing like this. JC was like a conductor, and their bodies moved with orchestrated precision. Mara and JC's dance was rapid and sensuous. He never gave a verbal command; still Mara met every turn, every move, as if they were one.

Eventually, the crowd stepped back to give them room. They clapped to the music. Mara and JC sambaed in one direction and then the other; and she felt as if her body were putty in his hands.

"You move like the women from my home city, Rio de Janeiro," he said in her ear as he stood behind her, directing her hips in a rapid shimmy.

"You aren't so bad yourself," Mara replied in a breathless way that had nothing to do with physical exhaustion.

Their eyes met.

"May I ask you something?" Mara ventured.

"Why, of course." His eyes seemed to gleam.

I have never looked into eyes this beautiful in my life, she thought. "Why did you ask me to dance?"

"I have two reasons," he replied. "The song you chose is very dear to me, and to someone that I love." JC swung her around. "Secondly, Roberto told me that you were the woman hiding under the hat that day, and that you were new to the samba. To see you dance the way you danced this evening, I had to congratulate you."

Mara laughed as she circled around him and

they took another twirl before the song ended. She saw Roberto and a group of men motion JC toward them.

"I think my time for pleasure is over." He looked deep into her eyes as he held her close. "I'm sure they've got some business for me to take care of. But I'll never forget this dance. Maybe you'll grant me the same pleasure at some other time."

"I'll look forward to that," Mara said.

They moved over to the sidelines. Mara watched JC walk away, but she continued to stand there as if she were in a trance. Her heart was beating fast and she could still feel his arms leading her body in the most fascinating, erotic dance. She saw a group of people close in around JC, and a cameraman take a shot with JC in the middle.

"Mara," Sharon exclaimed. "You danced with him. You two were beautiful together."

Mara looked at Sharon but she couldn't say a word.

"Are you okay?"

"I think so," Mara replied, and they erupted into laughter. Mara knew, Sharon saw, exactly where she was coming from. "Gir-r-r-rl," Mara finally said.

"You can say that again." Sharon nodded.

"Excuse me, I need a quick picture of you and the three other winners in the intermediate category," a photographer interrupted them.

Mara glanced over at JC. He was in the midst of being photographed again. "Sure," she said.

Sharon moved aside and Mara joined the other winners as they held their trophies. Afterward Sharon returned, and so did James.

"Hey. It's me again." James smiled.

"Hi, me," Mara replied.

James looked around. Mara watched his gaze rest on JC.

"Look, maybe we should get together and talk about some things."

"Like what?"

James pulled at the tip of his nose. "You know, the way we parted . . . I don't know if we ever really talked about it."

Mara paused. "I think enough was said." Her point was clear. "See you around, James." She looked at Sharon. "Ready to go?"

"If you are."

Mara took her belongings from Sharon's arms. James didn't budge. She glanced at JC. He was deep in conversation.

The crowd was streaming out of the gymnasium, so Mara, Sharon and James joined them. Mara turned one last time to catch a glimpse of the man who'd given her the best dance of her life. He looked over at her and smiled. Mara smiled, too, and left.

Chapter 7

"Gir-rl. Wasn't that something else? And you . . . you were just great." Sharon beamed. "I thought, 'Oh my God. Look at her go!' I was so excited for you, Mara."

"I did good, didn't I?"

"You did good. Yes, you did."

"I don't know what happened. At first I froze." Mara touched Sharon's arm. "Then I decided to just let go and I gave it all I had. And Sharon, this is an experience I will never forget."

"Me either," James said from behind them. "I'm really glad that you invited me, Mara." He held the door open and then slipped his arm around her.

"I didn't know she invited you," Sharon said.

"Mara knew when she told me about this that I wouldn't miss it for the world. How could I miss my girl's debut?"

"It wasn't my debut, James. I've been in a few interpretive dance recitals, and I told you about them."

"But this was different." He waved his hand. "I couldn't get to the others. I was tied up with work. But I was determined to come here and support you tonight."

They started across the street.

"Excuse me. Wait." A male voice hailed from behind.

Mara, James and Sharon turned as a man walked rapidly toward them. He stopped in front of Mara.

"JC asked me to extend an invitation to you and your friend." He looked at Sharon. "A few people will be joining JC tonight." He pointed toward the stretch Lincoln Continental. "Among other things they will rehash the contest and maybe enjoy a little champagne. JC wanted to make sure that you were one of the people that he invited."

Mara felt James's grip tighten on her waist. She looked at Sharon. She was smiling from ear to ear.

Mara thought about it for a moment. "You tell JC that I'd love to come."

"But Mara," James protested, "I wanted to invite you out to have a drink. I told you we've got things to talk about."

"But you never asked me." Mara smiled sweetly. "Now I've accepted this invitation."

"I'll let JC know," the man said. "He should be coming out shortly. And the limousine is available whenever you're ready."

"Thank you," Mara said, feeling important.

They watched him go over to the limousine driver and say a few words before he went back inside the building.

James removed his arm from Mara's waist. "I don't know what to say. You and I have been together for a couple of years. I'm trying to smooth things out between us, and you're not cooperating at all." He shook his head. "I really can't appreciate how you're treating me . . . us, Mara."

She looked at him. "James, there is no *us* at this point. And how I feel is that perhaps you have a small understanding now of how I felt every time you did the things you did. So I'm not going on the guilt trip you're trying to take me on."

He looked her up and down. "Okay. I see how it's going to be. But you remember this. When your fancy JC is done with you and he's not playing around on the other side of the tracks, then you call me."

Sharon's jaw dropped.

Mara squinted. "Even if I was thinking about it, you just made sure that I never will."

James's expression turned hard before he walked away.

Sharon grimaced. "Don't listen to him." She touched Mara's arm. "Come on. He's just jealous. And he's angry. But I say good for him, now the shoe is on the other foot."

"Yeah." Mara put her hand over her heart. James's words had hit their mark. "But it is kind of strange that JC is inviting us."

"Why not?" Sharon retorted. "What's wrong with us? And look at you. Tonight you look like a great samba queen. So you should be treated like one. Don't let James rain on your parade. He's just trying to hurt you. Don't even think about what he said. If JC had wanted to invite another woman, he would have. But he chose you, and that's because he knows a gem when he sees one. He's been all around the world and has enough money and women to know a good thing when he sees one.

It's obvious there is something about you that attracts him."

"And he's got a special affinity for the song that I chose for my performance," Mara replied.

"See there." Sharon snapped her fingers several times. "Something's clicking between you two on a whole different level."

They walked over to the limousine. The driver was leaning against the car.

"JC invited us to join him tonight. We were told we can wait for him," Mara said.

"Yes, you most certainly can." He walked over to the first passenger door and opened it.

Mara slid inside with Sharon right behind her. They sat and looked around the dimly lit interior.

"Look at this thing," Sharon cooed. "It's beautiful. Is this cherry wood?"

"It looks like it." Mara ran her hand over the panel. "It's gorgeous, isn't it?"

"Yeah," Sharon replied. "Everything in here looks brand new."

"It sure does." Mara leaned her head back against the high seat. "But the truth is, this is my second time being inside a limousine. The first was during my mother's funeral, and I was so sad I wasn't aware of what the car looked like inside."

"Well, I've never ridden in a limo," Sharon confessed. "But here we are." She looked around again. "What's that over there?"

"Looks like peanuts and something to snack on," Mara replied. "There are also some small pieces of fruit, like toppings for mixed drinks."

"That's probably what they are, because you know there's a bar in here," Sharon said.

"Of course there is. And look at that TV and stereo." They examined the gear.

"Eight people can sit in here comfortably."

"I know," Mara nodded.

Sharon balled up her fist and closed her eyes. "I have died and gone to heaven."

They started laughing, but one of the doors opened and the laughter stopped. JC climbed in and sat beside Mara. Roberto and another man got in and sat down with Sharon between them.

"I hope we didn't keep you ladies waiting too long," JC said.

"No," Mara replied. The scent of his cologne was heady. "We haven't been here very long. Not long at all." She couldn't hold his gaze in the confined quarters.

"We were looking around admiring the scenery." Sharon ran her hand over the cherry wood.

"You like it?" JC's voice was rich and deep.

"I think it's gorgeous," Sharon replied.

"And you?" He looked at Mara.

"What's not to like? It's beautiful." She folded her hands, uncomfortable under his stare.

His cell phone interrupted them. "Would you excuse me, please?" Mara nodded as he removed a tiny, slim phone from his pocket. "Hello. Oh . . . hello, Cat." He launched into Portuguese.

Mara glanced at JC when it was his time to listen, before he went into another session in his native tongue. Finally, Mara heard him say, "But he's okay. So everything should be fine now. No, don't worry. Thank you, Cat. *Ate logo.*" JC closed his cell phone and looked at everyone. "Sorry about that. I believe we were talking about the limousine."

Mara could tell from how easily he handled the situation that he was accustomed to socializing under these circumstances.

"It is a nice vehicle," JC continued. "And it makes traveling a little more comfortable."

"I'll say," Sharon replied.

JC smiled. "First, let me introduce Gene." He motioned toward the muscular dark-skinned man seated next to Sharon. "And of course you know Roberto."

They both nodded before Sharon offered her hand. "I'm Sharon." She smiled.

"And I'm Mara." Mara waved from the opposite seat.

"Mara," Roberto said with emphasis. "Our winner! You were beyond what I expected. You made every man in the place drool with desire with your dance."

"Don't start, Roberto." Mara shielded her eyes, but she could feel JC watching her.

"Well you did," Roberto insisted. "My God, woman, some of that stuff you did out there I've never seen before. Where you been hiding? You've been holding back on me." He leaned forward and grabbed both her hands. "Even though I advised you to get into the competition, I had no idea you could do all that."

"Neither did I." Mara laughed.

"And we are going to celebrate your win together," JC said. "We'll drive around, have a few drinks, and maybe pick up something to eat. Have a kind of rolling party. What do you say to that?"

"Sounds safe enough," Mara replied.

"Safe?" JC looked deep into her eyes. "After a performance like that, I would think you were not the kind of woman who plays it safe."

Chapter 8

Mara looked at Sharon as the limousine pulled away from the curb. She wondered if James was right. Perhaps her performance had given JC the impression that she was easy pickings. But Sharon appeared to be oblivious to Mara's attempt to catch her eye. She was too busy soaking up all the male energy.

"So where are we going?" Roberto looked at JC.

"I was going to ask you the same question," JC replied. "This is your town, man. Tell me, where are we going?"

Roberto smiled. "O-okay." He looked at everyone. "I say let's make this an international affair."

"What?" One of JC's dark brows lowered.

"I mean let's go somewhere that's got an international flavor. We can start with the Bahama Breeze."

"The Bahama Breeze," JC repeated. "Mara, do you know anything about this place?"

"Yes." Mara was caught off guard. "I've been there a few times."

"What is this face?" JC asked. "You didn't like it?"

"It's not that." She paused. "I guess I never envisioned taking a limo there."

JC looked at Roberto. "Are you steering me wrong, Roberto? Is this some kind of dive that you want us to go to?"

"No," Roberto said. "It's a cool place. I like the Bahama Breeze."

"It's fine," Mara spoke up. She didn't want JC or Roberto to think she was unappreciative.

"Are you sure?" JC questioned.

"Yes." *I must look like a total idiot now.*

"Okay," JC said. "Since Roberto thinks this Bahama Breeze is a good idea, let's do it. But let's call in and tell them to have everything ready. We can eat in here."

"But part of the fun is sitting on the decks with the colorful tiki lights," Roberto pressed.

"I say let's eat in here." Sharon sided with JC "I've never dined in a limo before." Her eyes sparkled, and Mara wished she could be as spontaneous and natural as her friend. "But that doesn't mean we can't enjoy the tiki lights. Let's park where we can see them and eat, too."

"That's a winner," JC said. "And since you chose the restaurant, Roberto, you are in charge of calling in the order."

"That's cool," Roberto replied.

He took out his cell phone and dialed information as Sharon started a conversation with Gene. JC turned to Mara.

"I'm glad you agreed to come. I wasn't sure that you would."

"Why wouldn't I?" she replied honestly. "Have you had many women turn down an offer to ride in a brand-new limousine?"

He laughed lightly. "Actually, I can't think of any."

Mara looked down at her hands. She folded and unfolded them.

"Are you from Orlando?"

"No, but I've lived in Florida all of my life," she replied. "I was born in Tampa. We lived there for awhile, and then my parents moved here to Orlando because my father found a better-paying job." She shrugged. "Nothing fancy about that."

"Hey." Roberto interrupted. "I'm going to order chicken and beef kebabs with pineapple. The beef has something called a pickapeppa sauce. I like to say that." He leaned toward Sharon and repeated "pickapeppa" in her ear.

She laughed. "Oo-oo. That tickles."

Roberto sat back. "How's that sound?" He looked at JC.

JC looked at Mara.

"Good." Mara smiled.

Roberto confirmed the order. "We're also going to have some yellow rice, and I ordered some fries."

"Sure," JC replied.

"But," Roberto got everybody's attention, "at the Bahama Breeze you've got to have some of their fancy drinks. They've got all kinds. Very tropical."

"We're all going to be sick tomorrow," Sharon commented.

"No you won't. If you're sick in the morning I'll fix you one of my famous concoctions. It'll knock that hangover right out of you."

Sharon leaned away from him. "Excuse me. If I'm sick in the morning, you won't be around to doctor on me."

"You never know." Roberto gave her the eye; then spoke into the cell phone. "What's the name of some of your drinks?" He announced the names of several piña coladas, margaritas, and a few others.

"Just get a couple of everything," JC said.

"Everything?" Mara laughed.

"I can be a little extravagant," JC replied. "Make that three drinks each."

"Now she's asking about dessert," Roberto said. "Anybody want some piña colada bread pudding?"

"I do," Mara replied.

"Me too," Sharon chimed in.

They looked at each other and laughed. Mara felt like a kid in a candy store. JC's extravagant approach to life made anything feel possible.

From the time they arrived at the Bahama Breeze and Gene brought the food and drinks to the limousine, the atmosphere continued to be light and jovial. It became even lighter as they consumed the tropical drinks. Mara never let on that she was not a drinker. As a matter of fact, she decided to turn over a new leaf. Mara picked up the piña colada and took a healthy swallow. Her gaze met Sharon's before Sharon took a sip of her own.

The ample drink was sweet and refreshing, and in no time at all, with a little rum under her belt, Mara wanted to know more about JC. "So how

long have you two known each other?" She motioned between JC and Roberto.

"I'd say more than twenty years."

"Really?" Mara was surprised.

"Yeah, it's been forever," Roberto said. "And it
feels like it."

JC chuckled.

"The truth is," Roberto continued, "he's like my
brother. So when I had the opportunity to come
here to the States, JC here took advantage of me,
and turned it into a business opportunity for him."

"You're so full of it, Roberto," JC replied.

"I learned it from the best," Roberto said. "And
as you can see, I'm taking advantage of the situation too." He leaned over as if he owned the limousine. "Now for the next phase of tonight's program,
we should go to City Walk. There we have all kinds
of possibilities."

"That's true," Mara replied. "I like Universal
Studios City Walk."

"Sold," JC said. "If Mara wants to go, I want to go
too."

Mara felt a little dizzy as she leaned close to JC.
"Are you trying to score points with me?"

His timbre lowered. "I certainly am. How am I
doing so far?"

"Very well," she said softly before she looked
away.

Minutes later they pulled up in front of the City
Walk entrance. Mara was particularly aware of how
close JC was sitting beside her. *Look what a piña colada and a half can do,* she thought as she closed
her eyes.

"We're here," Sharon announced.

"We're here." Mara looked through the window.

Suddenly, she looked down at her clothes. "But I can't go in there dressed like this."

"You look fine," Roberto said.

"You don't understand." Mara jiggled her fingers and laughed. "I-I" Mara tapped her chest, "can't go in there like this. Everybody's going to be looking at me."

Sharon leaned forward and touched her knee. "You've got your pants that you wore to the competition in your bag, right?"

"Yes," Mara said slowly.

"And how much did you have to drink?" JC hid a smile behind his hand. "I don't think it was even two glasses."

"That's none of your concern," Mara replied, bright eyed. "My concern is," she leaned toward JC, "walking in there, to the bathroom, dressed like this so I can put on my pants."

"That's no concern at all." JC made his face serious. "What we'll do is get out of the limo and you can turn it into your private dressing room."

"Really?" Mara looked stoned.

"Really." This time JC did not hide his smile.

Mara patted his cheek. "You're a kind man."

He patted hers in return. "I want you to remember that." JC opened the limousine door. "Let's let Mara change."

"I'm going to stay behind and help." Sharon looked at her friend's glassy eyes.

Roberto and Gene got out. Before he followed, JC whispered in Mara's ear, "Do I have to promise not to peek?"

Mara clicked her tongue in response. She attempted to whisper in his ear, but her lips touched his earlobe repeatedly. "You are going to be a problem in more ways than one. I can tell."

JC looked in Mara's totally smitten face. "I hope so," he said before he closed the door.

Chapter 9

Mara sat back and grinned at Sharon.

"You and piña coladas do not mix," Sharon said.

"He is heavenly," Mara replied.

"JC may be heavenly, and he is definitely after you," Sharon said. "And from the way you're acting, I don't think you should have drunk more than one piña colada."

"Don't be ridiculous," Mara replied. "I'm fine." She removed her pants from the bag. "But I tell you, I have never in my life felt like this before. I feel as if he has hypnotized me." Mara fell back against the seat.

"Yeah, you look like you're in another zone every time he looks at you."

"Don't tell me that." Mara removed her skirt. "Am I that obvious?"

"Are you?" Sharon rolled her eyes.

"I can't be that obvious. What is he going to think of me?" She ran her hand over her hair.

Sharon shrugged. "I think it's a little late to be

worried about that." A slow smile spread across her face. "It's pretty exciting, huh?"

Mara closed her eyes. "Exciting doesn't come close to how I feel." Her eyes opened slowly. "But, Sharon, I don't want to be too easy. My mother always said a man loves a challenge."

Sharon made a face. "Well girlfriend, you might need to work on that."

Mara's eyes beamed concern. "Oh, no. He probably thinks I do this all the time." She wagged an overactive finger. "And you know he thinks he's going to get laid tonight."

"I don't know what he's thinking . . . but I'm sure a man like JC doesn't get turned down too often."

"Yeah, I'm sure." Her eyes narrowed. "But I'm going to make him remember Mara Scott." She raised her arm as she rallied. "I'll be the one who held out to the last." Her body caved in. "But he's so handsome, and so smooth, and I can tell he wants me. This is better than any daydream I've ever had." Mara smiled a silly smile as she put on her pants.

"And, see, that's the point." Sharon picked up Mara's skirt and folded it. "This is not a dream, so you are in control. And what I say is, have a good time. This kind of opportunity comes once in a lifetime. Enjoy what he offers you, and don't do anything you don't want to do. You're a smart woman. At least you are the majority of the time," Sharon added under her breath.

"The funny thing is I never thought I'd be in this position. It's like the man's after the gold." Mara shook her head. "I never would have imagined a change of clothes and wearing contacts and makeup would make such a big difference. Look how James was acting."

They both laughed.

Mara's head spun as she pulled on her top. "But there is one thing I'm sure of."

"What's that?"

"No more drinks," Mara replied.

Sharon looked at Mara's glassy eyes. "That's one thing we can agree on. You ready?"

"Ready." Mara nodded.

"Now throw all that stuff out of your head. Keep your guards in place, but don't get stiff, Mara. I know you. Don't you go stiff on me."

"Stiff? I'm so far from stiff." Mara took a deep breath of air before she opened the limousine door.

"I was beginning to think you were going to stay in there," Roberto said.

Sharon slapped his arm.

"This is for you." JC unscrewed the top of some bottled water and handed it to Mara. "After all that dancing, your body needs water."

Their gazes held, and Mara knew that wasn't the only reason he was giving the water to her. "Thanks." *He is a nice man.* She accepted it and took a long drink.

Minutes later the group entered the crowded City Walk. JC walked beside Mara. Roberto walked with Sharon, and Gene trailed behind. The water and night air did Mara good. Her head seemed to clear a bit, and JC's kind gesture remained in her mind as they explored.

"He-ey. There's Emeril's," Mara said. "I love Emeril's." She grabbed JC's hand. "Come on, let's take a look inside."

He allowed her to lead him. "This Emeril, you know him?"

"Of course."

JC looked at the building with renewed interest.

"I watch his cooking show on television all the time."

"I see." JC stood behind Mara as they looked inside the restaurant. "Do you cook?" he said close to her ear, his body almost touching hers.

Mara's eyelids wavered. "Yes. Yes, I like to cook. I'm not one-eighth as good as Emeril," she joked, "but perhaps when you come back to the States, I can invite you to dinner one evening." She waited for his answer.

"I am open to all kinds of possibilities," JC replied.

That was a loaded answer, Mara thought as they joined the others and casual conversation began to flow.

In Mara's mind, Roberto took the crown for the group extrovert. He talked and cracked jokes constantly. When they reached JB's Margaritaville, Roberto had to stop in for another drink, and it was Roberto who piped up again when they reached the Latin quarter: "Hey, folks! We have arrived, and I think it's time to dance." He grabbed Sharon by the waist with one hand, held on to his lime margarita with the other, and took a couple of turns. Afterward he downed the drink in a matter of seconds.

Mara didn't want to think of dancing. By now the piña colada was wearing off and her feet were killing her.

"You must really like those drinks." Sharon put her hand on her hip. "Now, how many was that?"

"Who's counting?" Roberto replied. "They taste good and I feel good while I'm drinking them."

"Most of the men I know don't drink tropical drinks. Especially the way you're drinking them."

"They don't?"

"No."

"So, what are you trying to say?" Roberto stood close to her. "That I'm not manly because I'm drinking piña coladas and margaritas?"

Sharon gave him a look. "What I'm saying is most of the men I know don't drink them."

"But I can tell what you're thinking." Roberto slid his arm around her waist again. "Why don't you give me an opportunity to prove how much of a man I am?"

Sharon removed his arm. "No way. And from the way you're acting, I think you've had one too many."

Roberto's demeanor changed. He became serious. "Why? Because I'm making a move on a beautiful woman that I've liked all along?"

Mara could see he took Sharon by surprise. She tried to give him the eye, but there was a definite smile about her lips. "I still think you've had one too many." But she continued to walk beside Roberto and allowed him to whisper something in her ear.

"I want to dance," Roberto insisted minutes later. "I can feel it calling me." He shook his shoulders.

"Oh my God. You are a clown." Sharon rolled her eyes, but Roberto shimmied his shoulders even more. "You just don't know what you look like."

"Yes, I do." He made a sensuous movement with his hips.

Sharon shielded her eyes. "I don't know him."

"I tell you what." Mara came to Roberto's rescue. "I'm open to dancing, but the only place I want to dance is the Motown Café. I want to hear some of my folks and my music."

Sharon stopped and put her hand on her hip. "You don't have no claim on Motown just because you're black. I love Motown."

Mara showed Sharon her hand and looked at JC. "Can you handle Motown?"

His reply was quick. "I can handle anything you put before me."

She held his insinuating look. "Right now it's the Motown Café, and I want to dance the dances from my old neighborhood."

"We're on our way." JC took her by the hand.

They walked past the City of Jazz as Wynton Marsalis's trumpet filled the air. When they arrived at the Motown Café there was a line of people waiting to get in.

"Aw-w shoot," Sharon moaned. "It's going to be all night before we can get up in there."

"Not necessarily," J.C. replied. "Let me handle this." He held on to Mara's hand as he moved through the crowd that blocked the doorway. Finally, they reached a woman who was taking names for a waiting list.

"All right, sir, I just want to let you know there is going to be a forty-five-minute wait," the young woman began.

"I can see that it is a very popular place," JC

replied, "but the truth is"—he eased his hand out of his pocket and placed a folded fifty-dollar bill inside her podium—"there are five of us, and we simply want to borrow your dance floor."

The woman looked down at the money. "You don't plan to eat?"

"Not one bite." JC smiled.

She picked up the fifty. "Be my guests."

JC motioned to Roberto, Sharon, and Gene before he led Mara inside. Gladys Knight was blasting "I Heard It Through the Grapevine," and JC was moving before they reached the polished floor. They found a tiny space in the crowd and JC dawned a dance face.

Mara laughed at his antics. He reminded her of any brother from the hood. "I think you think you know how to dance."

"You think Americans are the only people that can do Motown?" he challenged. "I was dancing to Motown wa-ay, way back."

"Wa-ay back in the day," Mara corrected him and laughed even louder.

"Whatever." JC started singing.

Mara looked at Roberto and Sharon, and although a rhythm-and-blues tune was playing, Roberto was doing his Latin moves.

"This isn't the samba, Roberto," Mara called.

"But am I keeping up with the beat?" Roberto made a lightning-quick turn and wiggled his hips. "I ask you, am I?"

Mara surrendered. "You definitely are."

"That's all I want to know." Roberto continued to work it with his eyes closed.

They danced another fast song, and finally the DJ put on Marvin Gaye's "Let's Get It On." Breathing a little harder, but nowhere near exhausted, JC pulled Mara to him. "Uh-oh. You're in trouble now."

Mara was glad to rest in JC's arms. She felt a little tired, and allowed him to lead her in the slow dance, and lead her he did. She sighed as they moved, but as the song continued to play Mara tuned in to the lyrics, and it appeared JC did too.

"A man doesn't have to say a word when he's got Marvin," JC whispered. "He knows just what to say."

"Yeah, he does," Mara replied.

"If I was to choose someone to speak for me tonight, Marvin would have my vote."

Mara didn't saw anything, and by the time the song ended she was overly aware of JC's hard body and his penchant for rhythm. She continued to allow him to hold her.

Chapter 10

"Do you want to go another round?" JC asked as they stood together.

"I don't know if I can," Mara replied.

"Why is that?" He looked down with smoldering eyes.

Mara knew he knew the reason. That he could feel it. But she replied. "I'm tired."

He held her a moment longer. "Okay, then it's time to go. Are you two ready to head back to the car?" JC called to Roberto and Sharon.

"Yeah, I've had enough," Sharon replied.

"You've got to be kidding," Roberto said.

"No, I'm not kidding. I'm tired," Sharon sighed. "I've had a long day. I need my beauty rest."

"Okay." JC looked at Mara. "I'll have the driver drop everyone off at home."

"That won't work," Mara replied, still aware of the pulsing energy between them. "Our cars are parked at the gymnasium."

"We'll go to the gymnasium then," JC replied.

As they walked back to the limousine, every once in a while, JC would slip his arm around Mara's waist or hold her hand. For him, perhaps, it was natural behavior when he was out with a woman, but for Mara it was highly unusual. James never did it, and when it came to men in her life, her relationship with James had been the most intimate.

It was obvious the energy level of the group had waned; and as they rode back even Roberto was a little less bodacious. In the limo, Mara was aware of JC's knee as it rested against hers, while Roberto continued to provide the entertainment for the group. Although sometimes, for Mara, his voice rose above comfortable levels, it didn't seem to bother Sharon one bit. Every once in a while Mara would look at JC, only to discover he was looking at her.

"Are we back already?" Roberto asked, his words a little slurred.

"Yes, we are. And from the way you sound, I don't think you need to drive home," JC advised.

"What are you talking about?" Roberto asked. "I can handle it."

"It's not a matter of you handling it," JC said. "I don't want it on my conscience that you drank all night with me and ended up wrapping your car around a tree."

Roberto shook his head. "Don't do me like this, JC."

"He's not doing anything to you, but telling you right," Sharon jumped in. "He's looking out for you."

"I don't need anybody to look out for me," Roberto replied. "I can make my way home."

For a moment Sharon appeared vexed before her face took on a pronounced change. "Roberto, would you do me a favor?" She stepped outside the vehicle.

"Sure." He followed her. "What?"

"Let me drive you home." She smiled at him sweetly.

Roberto stopped weaving. "You'd do that for me?"

"Of course I would." Sharon looked away from his serious gaze. "You are one of the best samba instructors. I'm like JC; I don't want to see you wrap your car around a tree."

"Is that the only reason?"

"Maybe." Sharon lifted her chin. "But you're not going to find out the answer to that question tonight. So are you going to let me drive you home?"

Roberto smiled. "I may be a little drunk, but I'm not stupid. It's a deal."

Mara moved across the limo seat toward the door.

"Are you riding with Sharon?" JC asked.

Mara looked back. "Yes, we rode here together."

"Since Sharon is driving Roberto home, you must ride with me and let the driver drop you off," JC replied.

Mara looked at Roberto, who gave her a glassy-eyed smile.

"Now you know I don't mind taking you home, Mara." Sharon made it clear that she was a safe haven. "Where do you live, Roberto?"

"On Baker Street, near the cultural center."

"That's not too far away from where I live," Sharon replied.

"Yeah," Mara said. "So in order to take me home you've got to drive completely on the other side of town." Mara gave Sharon an in-control look. "I'll take JC's offer." She looked back at JC. He was sitting comfortably on the smooth leather seat.

"Are you certain?" Sharon pressed. "I don't mind."

"No, just go ahead," Mara assured her.

"Okay," Sharon replied. "Well, good night, JC. It was great hanging out with you."

"Same here," JC said.

"See you next time you're in Orlando, bro," Roberto's last word dragged.

Sharon put her arm through his. "You come on, but if we're going to start hanging out together you're going to have to bring it down a notch."

Mara smiled as Sharon took over. "Good night, Sharon. Roberto."

"Goodnight," they called as they walked away.

Mara closed the door and sat on the seat opposite JC.

"Now it's just the two of us," he said.

"So it is." Mara looked at him.

"How far away do you live from here?"

She looked down before fixing her eyes on his again. "It takes about twenty minutes."

"Twenty minutes," he repeated, and it sounded to Mara as if JC were calculating what could be done in that time. "Okay. You need to tell the driver where to take you."

"And how do I do that?" Mara looked around.

"That is an intercom button," JC pointed out. "Press it, and he'll be able to hear whatever you say."

Mara pressed the button. "Hello?"

"Yes, ma'am?"

"Can you take us to 1129 Colton Street?"

"I most certainly will."

Mara released the button, then pressed it again quickly. "Thank you."

"No problem," the driver replied.

The vehicle eased away from the curb as Mara and JC sat looking at each other.

Finally, JC said, "Why don't you come back over here and sit beside me?"

Mara shook her head slowly. Her body was one big tingle. "No, I think I'm fine just where I am."

JC continued to stare directly into her eyes. "Are you going to deny me the pleasure of spending these last few minutes beside you?"

Mara lifted a brow. "I'm not coming over there, that's for certain."

JC nodded. "Then I'll come to you." Smoothly, he changed sides and laid his arm across the back of the seat behind Mara's head. "Now, this isn't so bad, is it?"

"It's not bad at all," Mara said softly.

"Then why did you make it such an issue?"

"I may be a little slow sometimes," Mara paused, "but I generally hold back from making dangerous moves."

"Dangerous?" JC gently stroked beneath Mara's chin with his index finger. "You see me as dangerous?"

"Very dangerous." Her lips trembled when she smiled. "Ve-ery dangerous."

He shook his head. "But it's not true. Just because I find you attractive, and you are attracted to me, it doesn't make me dangerous."

Mara looked at him from beneath her lashes. "You don't waste any time in calling it like you see it."

"Why should I? We're grown people, and I think not speaking the truth at this point would be a waste of time. And time," he rubbed the back of his hand down Mara's face, "is ticking away. A twenty-minute ride is not very long."

Mara exhaled. "It's according to how you look at it. All sorts of things have been accomplished in twenty minutes."

"Yes, that's true." He kissed her on the cheek. "Your skin is beautiful. It is the color of peanut butter."

Mara's eyes rolled. "Peanut butter?"

"Yes," JC confirmed. "You don't like peanut butter?"

"I did when I was a kid," Mara laughed.

"I loved it when I was young. It was a lifeline for me." He kissed her cheek again. "But I don't remember it being this thrilling."

Mara chuckled. "You are something else."

"Would you like to know more about me?" He turned her chin toward him and pecked Mara on the lips.

"That depends." A second kiss cut off her words.

"And your lips are beautiful, too." Another kiss followed. "Full and oh-so-soft. God, a man could loose himself in such a mouth."

Mara began to feel lightheaded but she continued to hold back. That didn't deter JC. He gave her another short, soft kiss. "I said a man could lose himself, if you would only kiss him back." He focused his gaze on her mouth.

With half-closed eyes Mara studied JC's eyelashes. They were long and dark.

"Just one kiss, Mara, for a man who finds you so beautiful. So alluring. Just one." He spoke close to her lips before he covered hers again. This time, as JC held her face gently, Mara's resistance broke.

"That is more like it," JC replied. He wrapped his arms around her and gave Mara a long, deep, awakening kiss. She heard a sound deep in his throat as their heads repositioned and the kiss continued. Mara knew she had never been kissed like that before, and there was no one who had been able to bring out the kiss that she gave JC. All of her senses were alive, and her heart beat something awful.

"You are so sweet. You are so sweet, Mara," JC said as he came up for air, then kissed her again. One arm tightened about her while his other hand rubbed her back. "It's such a shame that we have only twenty minutes to get to know one another. I would love to spend much more time with you. You bring out something special in me."

Mara trembled as he kissed her again and again. JC's lips moved to her ear and he said something in Portuguese. Mara's eyes closed and she floated on a drunken wave of arousal as JC's hand lowered. He stroked her knee and then her thigh. Mara shivered as the vortex between her legs contracted and released.

JC's hand gently stroked Mara's neck before it grazed Mara's breast. "Desire is something, isn't it Mara? It is not easily controlled." He said between heightened breaths. "And you see, I cannot help that I want you. This desire is beyond me." His tongue sought hers. "What do you feel, Mara? Do you desire me?"

She dared not answer.

"Speak to me, Mara. Tell me if you want me."

At that moment, with all he had awakened in her, Mara could not lie. "Yes. Yes, I want you." She said, and JC's hand touched her breast. A shock of pleasure shot through her, and Mara realized the limousine had stopped. She opened her eyes. "The car has stopped," she said against his lips.

"I know," JC replied. "But that doesn't mean we must." He kissed her again, but Mara fought the wave of passion that threatened to take her over as they sat outside her family home. "But we have to." She pressed her hand against JC's chest.

"Must we?" JC asked through passion-filled eyes.

"Yes." Mara held firm.

JC exhaled and sat back. "This time twenty minutes was not nearly enough." His gaze swept over her.

"From where I sit, it was." Mara straightened her top and tried to take control of her breathing.

JC chuckled. He held her chin between his thumb and index finger and pecked her on the lips. "I will not forget you, Mara. You have touched me here." He covered his heart. "And when I return to the States, I will get in contact with you. Would you like that?"

Mara gave him a look that said he knew the answer to that question. "I'll wait for your call." She opened the car door. "Good night," she said as she recorded in her mind how enticing JC looked inside the limo.

"Good night, Mara."

Chapter 11

"Good morning." Mara smiled at the receptionist.

"Good morning to you. You're looking mighty
happy this morning."

"As a matter of fact," Mara couldn't help but
laugh, "I'm feeling rather good."

"I wish I could say the same." The receptionist
made a sour face.

"What's wrong?" Mara knew she shouldn't ask
Cindy this question. Cindy was nice but overly talk-
ative. But because of a wonderful night Mara was
feeling generous.

"I tell you." She exhaled. "More man trouble."

"Oh no," Mara said. She deliberately appeared
distracted by another employee approaching them
from the hall, but Cindy didn't appear to notice.

"Yeah. I don't know what I'm going to do. I've
mentioned Sam to you before. He just . . . My
goodness, I don't know. I've done everything to let
him know that I love him."

Mara looked at the hall again. This time it was vacant.

"What do you think I should—"

"Cindy." Mara showed the receptionist her palm. "I'm sorry." She leaned in. "Maybe we can talk another time, but I've got to get to the conference room. I have an important meeting this morning."

"Oh." Cindy looked disappointed.

Mara tried to lighten the situation. "Have you seen any stodgy, old business types come in?"

"Not really." Cindy looked as if she was trying to remember. "About fifteen minutes ago a couple of guys came in. I think I've seen one of them before, but they asked for Darlene."

"Darlene?" Mara shook her head. "No, I don't think the people I'm expecting would be asking for Darlene."

"Plus these men weren't old and stodgy."

Mara winked. "Another indication it wasn't them. Well, I better go."

Mara hummed as she headed for the conference room. She opened the double doors and stepped inside.

"There you are." Martin, Mara's immediate boss, greeted her.

"Good morning, Martin."

"Good morning. And I see you've got on your my-idea-is-going-to-prevail black suit."

"You're absolutely right." Mara smiled.

Martin sat down at the conference table. "It doesn't matter what you're wearing today and how psyched up you might be. It's not going to make a difference."

"Why?" Mara's brow creased.

"I don't know why we're even having this meeting."

"To wrap things up," Mara said. "And from my point of view there is still a slim chance that Jairo Incorporated will keep those indigenous trees in the design."

"The trees are out." Martin straightened a couple of files against the tabletop. "Look." He pointed toward the scale-sized model. "I was told to remove them."

Mara walked over and stood in front of the miniature building. The tiny trees lay on the side of the structure like discarded drink decorations. "What happened?"

"Darlene."

Mara tried to remain calm because now she could see Martin was pretty angry. "What's Darlene got to do with this?"

"Plenty it appears, although she's VP of finance and I was hired as manager of design." He folded his arms.

Mara just looked at him. She didn't know what to say.

"She came in my office all in a hurry," Martin continued, "and said 'We need to make sure we're positioned to do more business with Jairo Incorporated.' " He screwed up his face. " 'They are a huge client, and they don't want the indigenous trees. That's that. It's not even to be discussed today. During the meeting go over everything, but exclude the trees. I want to make sure that Jairo Incorporated is happy.' Then she said, 'You got that,' with that superior look that she can give you."

"But are design decisions Darlene's jurisdiction?" Mara was dumbfounded.

"Obviously, she feels they are. And that's what pisses me off. I am the head of the design team on this project. You and Beverly and I put in the hours and made this project what it is. You two have worked very hard, and I feel I've done a damn good job managing." His eyes spit fire. "I thought the design we produced was a beautiful one. We gave them some alternatives, and it's not that I am opposed to the trees being removed, but for Darlene to come in and tell me to do it! What's the point of my job if she can just come in and do this?"

Mara shook her head. "Where is Beverly?"

"She's coming. She's making copies of the papers that include this abrupt change."

Mara walked a few feet away before she turned and faced Martin again. "Being a finance person, does Darlene realize that by keeping the trees that it will save Jairo Incorporated all kinds of money?"

"I don't know what she knows." Martin threw up his hands. "All I know is she's got that Mr. Timor and some other guy in her office and the—" The double doors opened, and Martin stopped talking.

"Good morning, Mara," the breasty Darlene said in her best business voice.

"Good morning, Darlene. Gentlemen," Mara said.

"Martin, I saw you a little earlier."

"Good morning," Martin said through a forced smile.

"Let's all have a seat." Darlene took charge. "We can get this over and done with rather quickly. I think things have been made clear." She looked at

Martin. "So let's finalize everything for Mr. Timor, whom you may remember."

"Yes, I remember Mr. Timor," Mara replied before giving Martin a sidelong glance.

Martin simply nodded.

"And this is Mr. Regents. I don't believe you've met him," Darlene continued. "His responsibilities at Jairo Incorporated are similar to mine here at Beyond View. He's one of their financial guys." She smiled ingratiatingly. "Now that the introductions have been made, I'll turn it over to you, Martin."

"Thank you." Martin stood up. "Mr. Timor, you've seen the model before. Mr. Regents, please feel free to examine our scale-sized model of the project while we're waiting for some fresh copies of the summary. Of course, we do use computerized images as well, but for us here at Beyond View, we like to give our clients something they can touch." Martin licked his lips. "As you can see, the architecture is futuristic, an approach to design that we know Rio de Janeiro loves. So we pursued that love with this project, for as you can see, this building feels as if it has wings, as if it is about to take off at any moment."

"It's really quite interesting," Mr. Regents said. "I like the design. I like it a lot. What is this area right here?" He pointed to the place where the trees used to stand. "Is this a courtyard?"

For a second Martin's eyes turned to slits as he looked at Darlene.

"Actually Mr. Regents," Mara spoke up "this is a plot of land that currently is filled with indigenous trees, trees that are a landmark of how Rio's natural environment is maintained. They are also natural symbols of what Brazil stands for in the world, its rainforest." She could feel Darlene's eyes cutting into her. "It's a beautiful plot of land, not very large. This land had been a point of contention. We were going to discuss if these indigenous trees should be kept or not. I, for one, am a proponent for keeping the trees for two reasons." Through her peripheral vision Mara saw Darlene cross her arms. "One, financially it would be to Jairo Incorporated's advantage, saving thousands of dollars. Thousands," Mara repeated. "You would not have to cut down the trees and clear the land. And—"

"But," Darlene interrupted, "at this point, Mara, it's obvious that Martin didn't have an opportunity to inform you that keeping the trees is no longer an option. The trees will go and—uh . . . that's that." Her eyes hardened.

Mr. Regents looked at Darlene. "And why is that? She's telling me that keeping the trees will save us thousands of dollars, but it's been decided that they will be cut down anyway. Can someone tell me why?"

Mr. Timor spoke in a rather low tone. "Jairo has simply said he doesn't want the rainforest to be incorporated into this project."

"Does he realize the financial benefits of keeping the trees?" Mr. Regent's eyebrows rose.

Mr. Timor glanced around the table before he spoke in a low voice to Mr. Regents. "I don't think he knows, and I don't think he really cares about it. But I do know Jairo does not want the trees."

"Well." Mr. Regents pulled on his nose. "Jairo instructed me to come and make sure that good financial decisions had been made here, and in good conscience I can't say cutting down the trees is a good idea. As a matter of fact, I'd like to see this on paper."

"I've got something you can look at, Mr. Regents." Mara opened her binder. "They are some computer-generated photos that include the trees." She passed the papers across the table to Mr. Regents. "In other words, this is how the project would look with the trees." She pointed. "And I'm sure Martin can provide you with whatever financial information you desire. But to help you visualize this even more, I'll put these back." Mara began to replace the model trees.

"I most certainly can." Martin began to thumb through his papers as well.

Mara could feel Darlene's eyes on her, but she continued to talk about incorporating the trees in the design.

Mr. Timor leaned toward Mr. Regents and spoke in a confidential tone that Mara could barely hear. "The last time we tried to advise Jairo about this tree issue, he simply cut us off and said it wasn't up for discussion. I'm telling you, he's totally against it."

The double doors opened again. Beverly entered the room with a man behind her.

"We're right in here, Mr. Camara," Beverly announced.

"Jairo," Mr. Timor exclaimed. "I'm glad you were able to make it."

"We sure are." Mr. Regents's serious face softened.

"Well, my breakfast meeting finished on time." Jairo Camara walked toward the table with a confident stride. "And I'm glad because I wanted to sit in on this final meeting." He smiled.

"Great," Mr. Timor said.

By now Darlene was out of her seat and walking toward Jairo with an outstretched hand. "Mr. Camara. How wonderful to actually meet you. This is quite an honor." She shook his hand vigorously.

"Why thank you. And you are?"

"I'm Darlene Bay, Vice President of Finance here at Beyond View. And this is our design team." She made a graceful sweep of her arm toward Martin, Mara, and Beverly.

Mara stood transfixed. She stared at Jairo Camara in his black suit and accessories that even a blind man would know cost loads of money, and Mara could not believe it was JC, JC that had taken her around in the limousine, JC of JC's Dance Studio.

Jairo nodded in their direction, but barely gave them a glance as he walked over to the model.

"This is Martin Ritz," Darlene continued. "He manages the team and this—"

"I thought I said these trees were not to be a part of this project." Jairo looked back at Mr. Timor.

"I know that's what you said, sir. We were just discussing that, and I was making it clear that the trees were out."

Jairo's abrupt words jarred Mara. The whole scene did. JC, or Jairo, was the man who stood against the one thing that was so important to her. Mara looked at the tiny trees, then at Jairo, and it appalled her that he didn't have the courtesy to wait until she and Beverly were introduced before he showed it was his money, and therefore he had the power to do whatever he wanted. But what was most clear to Mara was that even though they stood no more than ten feet apart, Jairo did not recognize her.

"Yes, we were discussing the trees, Mr. Camara." Mara couldn't keep quiet. "And I was informing Mr. Regents about how keeping these indigenous trees as part of the design would save your company thousands of dollars."

"I'm not interested in saving money when it comes to this." Jairo looked at her.

Mara's heart pounded. She waited for him to recognize her, but he never did. Mara was further inflamed. "Are you interested in saving the environment, Mr. Camara? Your city? Your country? This world would not be what it is without the indigenous trees. There was a time when there were so many trees cut down from what is now Tujuca National Park, in Brazil, that it adversely impacted your environment to such a degree that they had to stop, and replanting was later initiated. These trees are important to what Rio is. To who you are, Mr. Camara."

Jairo turned to Darlene. "I thought you said he was the manager of the design team." He pointed at Martin.

"He is, Mr. Camara. I'm sorry."

Jairo positioned himself just enough to indicate his unreceptive feelings toward Mara. "I didn't come here to hear someone tell me the importance of the rainforest. And I don't want those trees to be a part of this project." He glanced at Mara. "Is there something difficult to understand about that?"

The edge on Jairo's voice cast a pall of silence around the room.

Mara looked down, then up again. All of her

happy feelings from the night before melted away. In confronting Jairo the businessman, the night before turned into a dream. Surely, the free-spirited man that she had spent the evening with would have shown a little compassion for a group of old trees, but most of all he would have recognized her.

"Yes," Mara nodded. "The position you have taken is very hard to understand, *Mr.* Camara. This is life." She pointed at the toothpick trees. "Trees like this provide life for all of those people in your city, and help to maintain life on this planet. And it is even more difficult for me to understand a mind dead set against them."

There were shocked looks around the table as Mara gathered her papers.

"Good morning, everyone," she said as she held her papers in her arms. "I guess my consulting work is done here." Mara glanced at Jairo before she started toward the door. She reached out to open it.

"Mara?" Jairo called.

She turned toward him, slowly. "Yes. Mara." She left the room.

Chapter 12

"Mr. Camara, I am so sorry." Darlene wiped her brow. "I just don't know what to say. Mara is a contractor here, and she's performed very well up until this point. Mr. Ritz, can you explain this?"

His eyes twinkled. "We knew Mara was an advocate for the environment. But we've never seen her like this." Martin tried not to smile.

"Well." Darlene exhaled. "I just don't know what to say about this . . . this display."

Jairo waved his hand before Darlene could go on. "It's okay. It's okay."

Silence encased the room.

"Would you excuse me for a moment?" Jairo didn't wait for an answer. He followed Mara outside. He saw her drinking from a water fountain down the hall. "Mara."

She stood up and wiped her mouth.

He walked toward her. "This is one of the strangest coincidences that I've ever encountered," Jairo began.

"Is it really?" Mara nodded. "Exactly what part of this are you referring to?"

Jairo stuck his hand in his pocket. "Seeing you here, in this environment, after being with you last night."

"I found that strange, too." She held her portfolio against her abdomen. "But the part that I found really strange is that you didn't recognize me."

Jairo's mouth tightened. "Yes, I did. It might have been a little late, but I recognized your walk as you walked away."

"Oh, so you recognized my walk, my body, but you didn't recognize my face. How thoughtful of you."

"Come on, Mara." He stuck his other hand in his pocket. "You do look quite different. Last night you had on lots of makeup and your hair was loose. Today . . ." His eyes searched her face intently. "You're not wearing any makeup. You have on black glasses and your hair is all pulled back. Anyone could have made this mistake."

"Anyone might have," Mara replied. "But not a man who claimed I made a big impression on him, that I touched him. Anyone else might have, but not a man who said those things, if," she raised her index finger, "he were telling the truth."

Jairo shrugged slightly. "I was telling the truth, Mara. You did touch me last night. And you're touching me now with your anger. It took a lot of guts to walk out because I did not recognize you."

Mara's chin lifted. "Is that what you think? The only reason I walked out of that conference room is because you didn't recognize me?"

"I think that was a big part of it." One smooth, black brow lifted.

"Once again you're wrong, Mr. Camara." She laced his name with sarcasm. "You're wrong. I walked out of the conference room because I had no idea how to deal with someone who was closed to something so important as the plight of the environment. But you absolutely did not want to hear it. And I just felt as if . . . the truth is, I didn't know what to say. And I was so confused." She shook her head. "You talk about not recognizing someone. The man I was with last night, and the one today," her hand swept between them, "there is no resemblance, even though you don't wear makeup."

"I am the same man, Mara," Jairo said. "But this is a different arena. Last night was the world of samba, of dance . . . emotion, wearing your heart on your sleeve, as you say in this country. But this is the business world, so I dress and act accordingly."

Mara's features hardened. "I don't need a lesson on the business world. I've operated in it for many years, and that's how I make my living."

Jairo surrendered her point with his hands.

"Okay, this is the business world," Mara continued, "but we presented a project to you that would save Jairo Incorporated, you, thousands of dollars, and you say no. Absolutely not."

He stared into her eyes. "Yes, I did say no, and that's what I meant."

Mara fortified herself against his sudden hardness. "But where is the business sense in that?"

Jairo's eyes turned hooded. "I understand the money aspects of it, but the decision that I made about those trees still stands. They must go." He

paused. "And I do not feel that I should have to explain that to you, or give you a reason why. We
hired your company to design something that we
could approve of. We approve of your project without the trees."

Mara looked down and nodded slowly. "Yes, and
as I said before," she looked up, "it is your decision. It is your money." Mara held her papers at
her side. "And now, I'm sure they are missing your
presence in the conference room. And I've got
something else to work on, if they will still have
me. Good-bye." Mara stuck out her hand.

Jairo took it and held on to it. "Good-bye? Just
like that?"

"That's the way it goes."

"Why, Mara?" His eyes softened. "Business is
business. I thought we had something on a personal level."

"I thought so too, last night. But now with this, I
know there's a huge gap between you and me. Not
only between our worlds, your being Brazilian,"
Mara shook her head, "you and your companies
and your money, but how we see the world. And
just like I've lost this battle, there is no need of my
fooling myself—I would be the one on the losing
end if I were personally involved with you. So I
want to spare myself the trouble. I'm old enough
to know how to do that."

"And you see me as trouble?" Jairo replied.

"I would say on a scale of one to ten, you are po-
tentially a big ten." Mara withdrew her hand. "I
need to go."

"So you don't want to stay in contact with me,"
Jairo said. "But I want to be in contact with you,

Mara. We just met, so how can you sum me up as a big ten for trouble so easily. I think we should—"

The conference door opened.

"Oh, there you are, Mr. Camara. I just thought I'd check to see what was going on. Everybody was getting a little concerned in there."

"Everything's fine," Jairo replied.

"He's coming, Mr. Timor," Mara said. "I was just about to go to my office. Good-bye, Mr. Camara." She nodded.

Jairo hesitated for only a second. "Good-bye."

Mara walked down the hall. Jairo and Mr. Timor went back into the conference room.

"Is everything okay, Mr. Camara?" Darlene inquired.

"Everything is just fine." Jairo smiled professionally.

"It appears you are familiar with Mara, our contractor." Darlene tried to conceal her disbelief.

"Yes." Jairo nodded. "We have met before, and because of that, in light of what had been said in here, I thought I would continue our conversation out in the hall."

Darlene donned her most businesslike manner. "I hope that Mara softened her stance, because truly, Beyond Vision understands that the client has the ultimate say-so when it comes to their projects."

"Well," Jairo said. "I'll say Mara and I understand each other better now than we did in the conference room."

"I'm glad to hear that," Darlene replied as Jairo took his seat. "Because Mr. Camara, we don't have room here at Beyond Vision for a contractor who would doggedly stick to their approach regardless of the wants of the paying client."

Jairo's brow lifted. "I hope that is not an implication, Ms. Bay, that you have no intention of using Mara as a contractor again, because if it is, then Jairo Incorporated would be forced to rethink its plan to use Beyond Vision for future projects." He smiled with a touch of venom.

Darlene sat back abruptly. "Oh. Absolutely not. Just the opposite. We welcome a contractor like Ms. Scott, a person with a vision beyond the rest of us sitting at this conference table. So we will definitely use her again, Mr. Camara."

"Good," Jairo replied. "And Jairo Incorporated will definitely come back to Beyond Vision."

Chapter 13

Nathan moaned as he pushed up from the easy chair. "I'm gonna go back here and make this phone call. That woman's called me twice." He glanced at Mara. "So I guess the least I can do is call her back."

Mara smiled slightly, but continued to look at the television. "Are you talking about Helen Davis?" she asked, although Mara knew the answer. *Even Dad's got someone who's interested in him. I'm the only one who can't seem to do that.*

"Um-hmm."

"You should definitely call her back, Dad." Mara glanced at him. "Anything else would be rude."

"Yeah." He ran his hand over his head as he walked toward the stairs. "That's how I feel."

Mara knew he was glad she was giving her consent. "I'm going to finish watching this movie before I go to my room and give myself a pedicure."

Nathan looked at the television. "It's taking too

long for them to get to the point for me," he remarked as he mounted the stairs.

Mara snuggled further into the couch cushions. She agreed the plot of the film was a little slow, but her interest peaked when a tall, dark-haired man came into view. He reminded her of Jairo.

Several days had passed and she hadn't heard a word from him. Mara couldn't pretend that she hadn't wished he'd call. She sighed and her eyelids closed. Despite Jairo's actions, Mara longed to experience how it might have been if Jairo had contacted her again. *If Jairo had come after her,* but this time the vision did not come. "But I'd love to experience it. I'd love to experience being with him again," Mara said softly. "Here in my house, on my simple turf."

Through her mind's eye and an imaginative ear, she heard the doorbell ring. *Mara got up and walked to the front door. She looked through the peephole and was stunned to see Jairo standing outside. Her hands began to sweat, but she managed to turn the doorknob and open the door.*

"Jairo."

"Hello, Mara."

"Hi-i." *She looked past Jairo to a parked, gleaming limousine, and across the street her nosy neighbor came out of her house and purposefully sat on her front porch.*

Mara looked back at Jairo. "What are you doing here?"

"I came to see you." *His eyes swept over her face.* *"Aren't you going to invite me inside?"*

Still stunned, Mara found the presence of mind to step back and open the door. "I'm sorry. I've forgotten my manners, but I'm so surprised to see you. I'm sure our house isn't anything like you're accustomed to but—"

Jairo stepped inside. He touched Mara's hand and

kissed her softly on the cheek. He looked around. *"Your house is beautiful, Mara. Just like you."*

She looked down as her face warmed with a sudden case of shyness. *"And you're sweet. Please, come in and have a seat."* She watched Jairo sit. He pulled his pants up just a tad. *"Would you care for something to drink?"*

He shook his head as his eyes remained intensely on her face. *"How have you been, Mara?"*

"I've been okay," she replied. *"And you?"*

"I've been good. Flying here and there. But my thoughts were always back here in Orlando, Florida, with you."

"Really?" Mara's forehead creased. *"I can't imagine a man like you, who flies all around the world, thinking about me."*

"But it's true." His dark eyes bore into her. *"I couldn't get you out of my mind. You've done something to me, Mara. I could never forget you. I would never want to."*

Mara looked up as her father walked into the room. *"Dad, I want you to meet someone. This is Jairo Camara. My father, Nathan Scott."*

"Hello." Jairo stood up and shook Nathan's hand.

Nathan simply looked at Jairo.

"Dad, I met Jairo, when I competed in the samba dance contest. Actually, the studio is named after him."

Nathan nodded. *"So you a dancer?"*

Jairo smiled. *"Yes, I am, Mr. Scott, among other things."*

"Oh, he's just being modest," Mara replied. *"Jairo is quite the businessman. I know of at least one other business that he owns, and from what I've heard he's quite a force in Rio de Janeiro."*

"Is that where you're from?" Nathan asked.

"Yes," Jairo nodded.

"And that's in Brazil, right?"

"Yes, it is, Mr. Scott."

"Well, I'll say." Nathan continued to stare at Jairo.

Jairo looked at Mara. "I just came by to let Mara know I was in town. To let her know I've been thinking about her."

"You got to come all the way to Orlando to find a woman to think about?" Nathan said under his breath.

"Sir?"

Nathan sat down. "Well I guess you better get going."

Mara's brow creased as she touched Jairo's arm. "Dad . . ."

"No, it's okay," Jairo said. "I do need to go, Mara." He stood up. He looked at Mara's father. "It was a pleasure to meet you, Mr. Scott."

"Good night." Nathan nodded.

Mara walked Jairo to the door. "It was really great to see you again."

They looked at each other.

"How did you get my address?" Mara asked.

"Roberto gave it to me."

Mara opened the front door. They walked out onto the front porch.

"Please," Mara's eyes softened, "don't hesitate to call me whenever you are in Orlando."

"Whenever I am here in the States, I'll give you a call." He touched her face.

Mara smiled. "Do you like to travel, Mara?"

"I think so." She looked pensive. "But I really haven't done that much traveling."

"Well, perhaps you'll consider making some trips with me."

"Where?" Mara's face brightened.

"Wherever the fancy might take us."

"We shall see." Mara looked down. "I'm a working girl."

"I know. But we'll work it out somehow. We must."

*Jairo took Mara's hand in his and squeezed it gently.
"It's good to see you, Mara."*

"The same here," Mara replied.

Their gazes remained locked as his face descended toward hers. Mara's entire body tingled as his mouth came closer and closer. And when Jairo's lips touched hers it became an exquisite kiss. Just for an electrifying second the tips of their tongues—

A large thud sounded upstairs, and Mara jolted out of her daydream. For a moment she was disoriented. "Is everything all right up there, Dad?"

"Yep. I dropped the telephone."

Mara pressed her fingers to her eyes. She thought of the daydream and her father's reaction to Jairo. "Now I can't even make things up the way I want them to be." Mara fought the sting of tears. "Another man. Another life of daydreams."

Chapter 14

"Sounds good, Julie," Mara said to her placement specialist. She looked through the window as she held the telephone. "I know you're on the job." Mara paused. "So you'll contact them and call me back?"

"I'll give you a call in a couple of days."

"Okay. I mean, it's only been three weeks since I completed my work at Beyond Vision, and I'm in great shape financially. Sometimes a little break in between doesn't hurt, huh?"

"No, it doesn't," Julie replied. "But don't get too comfortable because we'll have you on another contract very soon."

"All right. Just give me a call. Bye."

"Good-bye," Julie replied.

Mara hung up the telephone and gazed out of the window.

"So they haven't found you any more work?" Nathan said.

"No, not yet." Mara pushed the chair back from the desk. "But I'm sure she will. She always does."

"Yeah but, you know, I don't know how you live like this, Mara. Not knowing from week to week if you're going to have a job or not. I hope you realize, if it wasn't for what I established while I was working hard and long in that factory, you'd be between a rock and a hard place."

Mara closed her eyes. "Dad, I appreciate what you've done, and definitely you've made my life very comfortable." She looked at him. "But I just don't see it the same way that you do. I've been contracting for five years and I've worked consistently. I haven't had any money problems over—"

"You haven't had any money problems because I pay for everything. My pension and my Social Security take care of all of the bills. What's going to happen to you when I'm gone? You need to find a husband."

Mara stiffened. "Dad, I've told you a million times that you don't have to pay for those things. I've tried to give you money for rent and for the bills and you won't take it. So please," Mara offered her palms, "it makes me feel bad when you talk like this."

Nathan looked down. He picked up the newspaper. "It's not my intention to make you feel bad. I just don't understand you young folks today, your personal life or how you work. In my day, you worked at a company, you stuck with it, and you were rewarded for your loyalty. But now adays you young people are looking for short-term gratification in everything, and I just think you have to pay for it in the end." Nathan shook his head.

Mara leaned forward. "And you did right for

your day, Dad. You're right. Look how far your pension and your Social Security goes. It can take care of us. But things aren't the same as they used to be. People are loyal to companies, and right before it's time for them to retire, the company gets rid of them. They fire the person, and then they hire someone younger than me who is willing to come in at a much lower cost. Things aren't the same, Dad, personally or professionally. And I just wish that you could accept how I've chosen to live my life and make a living, just as I have been able to be truly grateful for all you've done through the years for me."

His shoulders jerked. "I tell you what, if your mother or I had chosen to work like you work, I don't know if there would have been food on the table every day. That's for certain."

Nathan bringing in her mother made Mara snap. "Maybe if mother had chosen to work like I work, if she'd had that option, she'd still be with us today. It was working in that place all those years, breathing in asbestos, that killed her."

The room went cold silent.

Mara shook her head. "Why did you have to bring mother into this? It seems like things always go downhill when we talk about her."

Nathan put down the newspaper. "So are you saying your mother worked in that factory because I couldn't support this family, and that's the reason she died of cancer? Is that what you're saying?"

"My God, Dad." Mara closed her eyes again. "Why do we torture ourselves like this? Mom's been gone for over two years now, but it's like we open up a sore whenever her name comes up." Mara paused. "Mom died of mesothelioma because she worked at an old factory that had asbestos in the walls and the air. That's it. I never said you didn't take care of this family, that mother had to work because you couldn't take care of us. And I've told you that a million times," Mara pleaded. "But no matter how much I try to reassure you of that, you still strike out at me at uncalled-for times, and in uncalled-for ways. And I end up saying things that hurt you." Mara sighed. "I'm so tired of this. And I think it keeps happening because you haven't let go of Mom. You're stuck in the anger part of the healing process."

"I don't want to hear about where I'm stuck." He slammed the newspaper down. "Yes, I might be stuck, but I was married to your mother for forty-six years, so how am I supposed to get her out of my system in only two years? Tell me that. You just don't know how I feel."

Mara looked down. "No, Dad. I don't know how you feel, and I'm not trying to say that I do. But I can say she was my mother and I loved her, too. And I'd known her all of my life." She wiped her nose.

Mara got up and walked into the kitchen. She opened the refrigerator, took out a pitcher of water; removed a glass from the cabinet, and filled it. Mara leaned against the cabinet and slowly drank the cold water. As she placed the empty glass in the sink, the telephone rang. She answered the outdated phone that hung on a wall nearby.

"Hello."

"Hello, Mara?" A male voice replied.

Her brow creased. "Yes, this is Mara."

"This is Roberto from JC's Dance Studio."

"Hi, Roberto." Mara tried to lighten her mood. "How are you?"

"I'm doing fine. And yourself?"

"I'm making it." Mara looked down.

"Well, I can guarantee you after this phone call you'll be doing better than that," Roberto said.

"Really?" Automatically Mara's mind went to Jairo. He had been on her mind more than she cared to admit.

"Really," Roberto replied. "You are one of the winners of the national drawing."

"What?"

"Yes! You are one of the winners!" Roberto repeated. "I am holding your tickets and accommodations for two to Rio de Janeiro."

"My God, Roberto. You've got to be kidding!" Mara said through a stunned smile.

"No, I'm not kidding. Not at all."

Mara touched her cheek. "When is this trip?"

"One month to the day."

Mara looked at the calendar that hung by the phone.

"We know that doesn't give much time, but we're hoping all of the winners will be able to come."

"I just can't believe it, Roberto." Mara was still reeling. "I've never won anything."

"That's not true. You won the dance competition, and now you've won a trip to Rio. So, call me back when you're ready to confirm."

"I will," Mara said. "I will."

"Great. You think you can let me know in a couple of days?"

"I think so." Mara began to laugh. "Oh my goodness! Thank you! Thank you, Roberto."

Roberto laughed too. "Talk to you in a couple of days."

Mara hung up the telephone. When she turned around, her father was standing in the kitchen doorway.

"Dad, you won't believe this."

His eyes narrowed. "What is it?"

"I won a trip for two to Rio de Janeiro, Brazil."

"Oh-h." He looked surprised, almost excited.

Mara noticed the spark of light in her father's eyes, and love for him flooded inside of her. "It's a trip for two, Dad. Would you like to go with me?"

Nathan's eyes grew even brighter, then Mara watched them slowly dim. "No. No, I don't think I'd like to go."

"Dad! Come on! You've never been outside of the States, and this is a free trip. It's scheduled one month from now. It'll be exciting."

"No, that kind of thing isn't for me." He shook his head. "I don't like flying no way, and going that far . . . ." He shook his head again. "That's just not me, Mara. And I'm too old to change." Nathan looked at Mara with a sad smile. "Thanks anyway for asking me. I'm sure you'll find someone else to go."

Chapter 15

Mara and Sharon walked out of the department store and into the common area of the mall.

"I can't believe you didn't buy that top." Sharon shifted her bags to her other hand. "It was you, Mara. It was really you."

"Well, I'm not actually working at the moment," Mara replied.

Sharon gave her the eye. "That's never stopped you before. And you always get another contract. Plus I know you." She wiggled her head. "You've probably got savings up the patootie. You're not like me. You save and you plan. So don't give me that. Something else must be wrong. You've been acting kind of funny ever since I picked you up."

"I really can't say anything is wrong." Mara sighed. "I had another confrontation with my dad. Just a small one, yesterday, and I guess it's kind of playing over and over in my mind. I could have reacted differently to what he said, but I just couldn't help it. At least I didn't let him drag me too far into the you-need-a-husband bit."

"Hey, don't beat up on yourself. You know I know your dad, and he's a good man. He loves you and all, but he can be a little rough sometimes." Sharon glanced at Mara. "He sees things his way, and anybody else's way, if it's not his, isn't right. So, hey, don't be so hard on yourself. I think both of you are still trying to deal with your Mom being gone. And I think your father is having a harder time of it than you are, which is to be expected."

"Yeah." Mara nodded. "And that's what I need to realize. I really do." She looked inside a bookstore. "Let's go in here."

"Sure," Sharon said.

They walked into the store. Sharon tagged behind as Mara explored the bargain books and the books against the walls. Eventually they wound up in the travel section.

"So how are you and Roberto coming along?" Mara asked.

Sharon burst into a smile. "We're doing pretty good. We went to the movies the other night and we had dinner at his place afterward. It was nice." Sharon focused on a bright book cover turned out for all to see.

"Wow," Mara replied. "Did he cook?"

"He did." Sharon's eyes glowed when she looked at Mara. "And it was really good. He cooked a couple of dishes that he said he grew up on. One was a black bean stew." She closed her eyes as if she were picturing it. "And when I say stew, oh my God, this stew was full of some of everything. Beef. Sausage. And he served it with some Brazilian rice that had onion and tomato in it. It was so good. I really was impressed."

Mara smiled. "I can tell."

"Can you imagine Roberto cooking with all his antics." Sharon continued to bubble over. "But, you know, after we went out a couple of times, and he cooked for me once before," she confessed, "he really wasn't the same guy that we saw that night when JC, I mean Jairo, was here." She made a slight face before she brightened again. "And he's different from the instructor image he puts on at the studio. I've kind of gotten to know Roberto the man, and he's pretty nice."

"I can tell you like him," Mara said. "I can also tell because I haven't heard from you much lately. I knew something was keeping you busy. I didn't know what."

Sharon looked guilty. "Come to think of it, I guess we have been out quite a bit. I-uh, I did call you a couple of times, Mara."

"I know. Please." Mara dismissed it with a wave of her hand. "It's no big deal. I'm glad that you and Roberto are really hitting it off."

"Are you?" Sharon leaned forward and looked into her eyes.

"Yeah, I am," Mara said, sincerely.

"Good." Sharon picked up a travel book and flipped the pages. "Maybe you and your dad should do something together. He never goes anywhere. He's worse than you, and you're pretty bad." She wrinkled her nose. "Maybe you all should go on a trip together. That might change his perspective a bit."

"Actually, I thought about that." Mara picked up a travel guide of Rio de Janeiro. "Yesterday I invited him on a trip, but he wasn't interested in going."

"Where did you want to take him? You know the man hardly goes across town, so you have to start off small with him. And I know you made it clear that you would foot the bill."

Mara looked at the color photos inside the book. "Yes, I told him it was all paid for, but that didn't seem to move him at all."

"Where did you want to go, to the moon? Because I can't believe that your saying you would pay didn't move him."

"No, it wasn't the moon," Mara replied. "It was Rio."

"Rio." Sharon's voice rose. "As in Rio de Janeiro?"

Mara placed the book back on the shelf. "Yep."

"I'm shocked," Sharon replied.

"I was shocked too when Roberto called me yesterday and told me I was one of the winners from the drawing."

"Roberto called you and told you that you were one of the winners of the drawing and he didn't tell me, nor did you call me and tell me?" Sharon accused. "I'm mad at both of you."

"Well, I was going to call you, but after my father's reaction and a few other things that kept going through my mind, I didn't want to think about it any more."

Sharon pulled her ear. "I must have not heard you right. You didn't want to think about what? Going to Brazil? Mara! Are you crazy?"

"No, I'm not crazy. But I didn't want to think about it, Sharon. I didn't," Mara said. "I didn't want to think about all that it means. The dancing, traveling there, who I would ask to go with me."

"You'd ask me," Sharon blurted. "Your best friend of the last ten years. Hello-o-o."

"Of course you are the best choice." Mara looked at her. "And I thought about that. But the truth is, Rio of all places at this point, just does not call to me."

Sharon put her hand on her hip. "Yeah, I bet it didn't. I bet it called to you too loudly."

"I don't know what you're talking about." Mara didn't look at her.

"You know *who* I'm talking about. You haven't gotten Jairo out of your mind. Not that he would be easy to remove. But I know that brought him up even stronger for you."

Mara's brow creased. "Yeah, it did. And he didn't leave the best taste in my mouth, Sharon." She shook her head. "I don't know why I can't stop thinking about him. It's just not like me. For days the competition and seeing him at the business meeting kept playing over and over in my mind. And then I'd wish that I'd flirted more at the end. Then I'd switch and think I said the right things. Then I'd change my position again. Then I'd think 'you know, you'd be nothing but a play thing for this man.' But I couldn't stop thinking about him." She stared at Sharon. "So this sensible woman that you know kind of went out of the window. And I didn't like that. And here, out of the blue, out of all the people who entered that contest, I end up being one of the winners."

Sharon looked down for a moment. "Look. Jairo Camara is . . . That man is so rich, and he's probably got so much going on in Rio de Janeiro and all over this planet, that the chances of your bumping into him in Rio are null and void. You've already said that you would be nothing but a play thing for this man. So, at this point, girlfriend, I hate to put it this way, but he's long gone. He hasn't tried to contact you, which he obviously could if he wanted to. He's somewhere flying around the world. He is not thinking about you. So what you need to think about is yourself. A free trip to Rio de Janeiro?" Sharon's eyes widened. "C'mon now. Rio de Janeiro. You'd love to go. Wouldn't you?"

"Yeah." Mara looked at her friend. "Normally, I would."

"Well, let's be normal," Sharon said. "Let's go. When is it?"

"About a month from now."

"Hey." Sharon literally put her foot down. "I work for the city. And I've got plenty of vacation time. Plus I've got sick days stored up, too. Mara, you can't pass up this opportunity. When will we ever get to go to Rio again? When?"

"But the truth is, Sharon, I've never had any desire to go."

"Desire or not. Rio . . . think about it. Some of the most beautiful people in the world live in Rio. I mean, my God, the men over there are like gods. Mara, don't pass up this opportunity," Sharon folded her hands in prayer, "for lust and adventure. At least that's what it would be for me."

Mara chuckled. "If Roberto could see you now." She looked down. "And when you put it that way, how can we not go?"

Sharon's eyes narrowed. "And I cannot believe that Roberto talked to me last night and didn't tell me that you had won."

Mara nodded slowly. "Well, I think that says the man has integrity."

"It does, doesn't it?" Sharon's expression turned reflective.

"Yep, and that's more than I can say for some folks." She thought of Jairo.

A couple of hours later Mara returned home. "Hey, Dad. I'm home."

"Hey."

She followed his voice to the kitchen. Her father was standing over the sink.

"I had a taste for boiled eggs," he said as he ran water into a small saucepan.

"That should hold you until I fix us something for dinner," Mara replied. "You've got anything in mind that you want?"

"No." He shook his head. "Not really. Whatever you fix will be fine." Nathan walked over and placed the pot on the stove. "Where've you been?"

"Sharon and I met at the mall and did more window shopping than anything else. Seeing as I'm not employed right now, I guess I should kind of hold back."

Nathan looked at his daughter. "Don't worry about the job thing, Mara. Don't even listen when I say some of the things I say. I'm just concerned about you. But overall," he patted her face, "you've been a good girl. A great daughter, and I don't want you to think you're anything less than that."

"Why, thank you, Dad." Mara's heart filled with love. "And you've been a good father, and I want you to know that too." She gave him a peck on the cheek.

"And just because I turned down your invitation to go on that trip with you, it doesn't mean you shouldn't go. It's quite an opportunity for a young person like you. You know, my exploring isn't going to go much further than this city, but it doesn't mean you shouldn't take advantage of something like that."

"I plan to, Dad. I told Sharon about it, and of course she was raring to go."

Nathan's eyebrows rose. "Sharon would be. Sharon is raring for everything. Talk about a zest for life." He placed the eggs in the pot.

"Yeah, she said she would go, so I've decided to go."

He turned on the fire. "Why shouldn't you? You won that prize. You deserve to go."

"Are you sure you're not going to be lonely without me?"

He waved his hand. "You know I can always find something to do around here. I'll find something to keep me occupied."

"Did you talk to Helen?" Mara asked.

"Yeah, I called her back."

"What did she say?" Mara glanced at him.

"She claims that she likes to fish. Although I don't know if she's just telling me that to get in good with me." He looked at Mara.

She smiled. "I think that she's a woman that can be trusted. We've known her for quite a while, and I'd take her out if she was willing to go."

Nathan looked pleased. "So when is your trip?"

"In a little less than a month," Mara said.

"Well, you go there, and you show those folks what Mara Scott is made of. And have a good time. Don't be like your Dad, an old stick-in-the-mud. I want more for you."

An Important Message From The ARABESQUE Publisher

Dear Arabesque Reader,

Arabesque is celebrating 10 years of award-winning African-American romance. This year look for our specially marked 10th Anniversary titles.

Plus, we are offering *Special Collection Editions* and a *Summer Reading Series*—all part of our 10th Anniversary celebration.

Why not be a part of the celebration and let us send you four more specially selected books FREE! These exceptional romances will be sent right to your front door!

Please enjoy them with our compliments, and thank you for continuing to enjoy Arabesque.... the soul of romance bringing you ten years of love, passion and extraordinary romance.

Linda Gill
PUBLISHER, ARABESQUE ROMANCE NOVELS

P.S. Don't forget to nominate someone special in the Arabesque Man Contest! For more details visit us at www.BET.com

A SPECIAL "THANK YOU" FROM ARABESQUE JUST FOR YOU!

Send this card back and you'll receive 4 FREE Arabesque Novels—a $25.96 value—absolutely FREE!

The introductory 4 Arabesque Romance books are yours FREE (plus $1.99 shipping & handling). If you wish to continue to receive 4 books every month, do nothing. Each month, we will send you 4 New Arabesque Romance Novels for your free examination. If you wish to keep them, pay just $18* (plus, $1.99 shipping & handling). If you decide not to continue, you owe nothing!

- Send no money now.
- Never an obligation.
- Books delivered to your door!

We hope that after receiving your FREE books you'll want to remain an Arabesque subscriber, but the choice is yours! So why not take advantage of this Arabesque offer, with no risk of any kind. You'll be glad you did!

In fact, we're so sure you will love your Arabesque novels, that we will send you an Arabesque Tote Bag FREE with your first paid shipment.

* Prices subject to change

THE "THANK YOU" GIFT INCLUDES:

- 4 books absolutely FREE (plus $1.99 for shipping and handling).
- A FREE newsletter, *Arabesque Romance News*, filled with author interviews, book previews, special offers, and more!
- No risks or obligations. You're free to cancel whenever you wish with no questions asked.

INTRODUCTORY OFFER CERTIFICATE

Yes! Please send me 4 FREE Arabesque novels (plus $1.99 for shipping & handling). I understand I am under no obligation to purchase any books, as explained on the back of this card. Send my free tote bag after my first regular paid shipment.

NAME

ADDRESS _____ APT.

CITY _____ STATE _____ ZIP

TELEPHONE ( )

E-MAIL

SIGNATURE

Offer limited to one per household and not valid to current subscribers. All orders subject to approval. Terms, offer, & price subject to change. Tote bags available while supplies last.

Thank You!

AN084A

ARABESQUE

Accepting the four introductory books for FREE (plus $1.99 to offset the cost of shipping & handling) places you under no obligation to buy anything. You may keep the books and return the shipping statement marked "cancelled". If you do not cancel, about a month later we will send 4 additional Arabesque novels, and you will be billed the preferred subscriber's price of just $4.50 per title. That's $18.00* for all 4 books for a savings of almost 40% off the cover price (Plus $1.99 for shipping and handling). You may cancel at any time, but if you choose to continue, every month we'll send you 4 more books, which you may either purchase at the preferred discount price. . . or return to us and cancel your subscription.

* PRICES SUBJECT TO CHANGE

THE ARABESQUE ROMANCE BOOK CLUB
P.O. BOX 5214
CLIFTON NJ 07015-5214

THE ARABESQUE ROMANCE CLUB: HERE'S HOW IT WORKS

PLACE
STAMP
HERE

"I know you do." Mara looked down.

"I want you to experience all kinds of happiness, including having a family. You know, the older I get, the more I think about grandchildren." He looked into her eyes. "Janet and I only had you, and recently I thought, if Mara doesn't have any children, where are we going to be?"

Mara studied her Dad's face. "Do you really think about that?"

"Of course I do. Children are our future. When your mother was sick, you took care of her so well. You were there when she needed you, Mara, and for me when I didn't know what to do. So I want someone to be there for you."

Mara looked at the uncertainty of her future. "People do get along without ever having children. I mean, I don't want you think I'm going to be some old lonely maid."

"It's not about that, Mara. I just want you to know what it feels like. I know some folks say children are more trouble than they're worth, but I don't think that's really true. And sure enough," a gleam entered his eyes, "I'd like to know what it feels like to be a grandparent. I know your mother wanted it. So I'm looking forward to some nice young man to take up with you, Mara, and want you for his wife. Every dad wants his daughter to get married to someone who really cares for her."

"Wow." Mara sighed.

"Well it's true. What about that James fellow? I haven't seen him lately. He used to come around quite often. I thought he was okay."

"Yeah. He was just okay." Mara rolled her eyes. "That's about all he was. We're not seeing each other," she hesitated then added, "right now." Her father's dreams of grandfatherhood stopped her from making it more permanent.

"Don't worry," Nathan said. "The right one will come along. I'm certain of it. A special woman like you needs a special man. The right one will come. I'd be willing to bet on it."

Jairo's face entered her mind, and Mara tried to push the image away as she kissed her father on the cheek again. "Well . . . we shall see."

Chapter 16

"Oooo! Look at that man, girl. Look at that man. Have you ever?" Sharon stared at a man with dark skin, wavy brown hair, and green eyes.

"All right, now. I'm going to report you to Roberto when we get back to Florida. Especially since he wants you to go by and visit his family while you're here."

"That's sweet of him, isn't it?" Sharon glanced at Mara. "I tell you, he's such a sweetheart now. But being with Roberto hasn't done anything to dim my vision." Sharon put her nose near the car window. "I can't help it. Everywhere I look, the Brazilian men are so beautiful, and the women are too."

"Yeah, Brazil's known for its beautiful people." Mara glanced at the crowds parading down the streets with skin in all shades of brown; hair of various colors, lengths, and textures; and eyes ranging from blue to black. "Rio is some city, huh?"

They took in the tall office buildings, the colorful restaurants, and a barrage of shops and stores.

"And here we are," Sharon settled back and crossed her legs, "riding in a car that was waiting for us with a placard. Girl, you know, JC's Dance Studio knows how to do things right. And it's obvious *they* have plenty of money to do it." She glanced at Mara. "And you know what I mean."

"Yeah I know." Mara continued to look out of the window.

"It's true. Jairo's got plenty of money. And you know what?"

"What?" With her eyes, Mara dared Sharon to say the wrong thing.

"We are taking advantage of it."

Mara thought about it. "We sure are." She sat back and crossed her legs too.

Sharon laughed. "Copycat."

A short time later the hired car pulled over to the curb.

"This is your hotel." The driver announced with a marked accent. "The Golden Tulip Ipanema Plaza, ladies. It is a wonderful hotel in a great location, just a block or so away from the beach, and there are many restaurants, clubs, and bars nearby, as you saw on our way here. Good shopping too. So welcome," he smiled, "to my wonderful city of Rio de Janeiro."

Mara marveled at his white smile. It gleamed against his dark, dark skin. "Why, thank you."

"And let me thank you too," Sharon chimed. "We're so happy to be here."

The driver opened the door for Mara and Sharon before he removed their suitcases from the trunk of the car and handed them to a bellboy. Mara paid him and gave him a tip.

He smiled again. "Please, I hope you have a pleasant stay in our city, and that you will come back again."

Mara and Sharon went over to the slender young man who was piling their luggage onto a luggage carrier.

"This way please," he said.

They entered the lobby. The furnishings inside the Golden Tulip had a definite contemporary feel, and it was obvious no expense had been spared. The hotel was abuzz, and Mara and Sharon did some people watching while they waited in the check-in line.

"May I help you, please?" A woman motioned toward the counter.

"Hello. I'm Mara Scott," Mara informed her. "And I have two rooms registered under my name."

"Let me check," the attendant replied as she entered the information into the computer. "I see you here, Miss Scott, and, um, yes, there are two rooms for you. Oh, but I'm sorry," she said. Mara and Sharon looked at each other with concern.

"I hope we didn't speak too quickly," Sharon whispered to Mara, "about JC's Dance Studio having it together. Lord knows we don't need any trouble all the way over here in Brazil."

"Something happened here," the attendant continued. "And as a result of a problem they had with the rooms, Miss Scott, you have been upgraded."

"Really?" Mara glanced at Sharon.

"Yes, ma'am. You are going to really enjoy the rooms that we have for you here at the Golden Tulip." She smiled. "There are two rooms and they are joined. There is a door that can be locked between them." She appeared to be reading. "But I can see that everything has been taken care of. Let me get your paperwork together, and you will be on your way."

Sharon leaned toward Mara. "Upgrade, I always love that word. Upgrade."

The attendant looked at them.

"Calm down," Mara said behind a concealing smile. "Let's try to act as if we have some level of sophistication."

"Sophistication." Sharon sniffed. "I don't know what you are talking about. I am the epitome of that."

"Then act like it." Mara tried not to laugh. "Right now you're acting as if you've never been away from home."

"I've never been to Rio before," Sharon replied.

The attendant returned to the counter. "Here you are. This is your room key, Miss Scott." She gave Mara a card key. "And I'm assuming the second room is yours."

"Yes, it is," Sharon replied.

"May I get your name, please?"

"My name is Sharon Vegas."

The attendant typed quickly. "Good. Now the bellboy will take your bags up to your rooms. And to get there, take the elevator." She pointed. "Your room numbers are seven fourteen and seven sixteen. Please enjoy your stay at the Golden Tulip."

"We most definitely will," Mara replied.

They walked over to the elevator and went up to the seventh floor. Mara and Sharon looked at the numbers on the doors as they proceeded up the hall.

"It's down this way," Mara said as they turned the corner.

They walked to the end of the hall.

"This can't be it." Mara looked at the plaque on the door. "This is the master suite!" She checked the room number.

"You've got the master suite." Sharon's eyes widened.

Mara slipped the card key into the door. "Oh my God," she said as she entered with Sharon behind her.

"You can say that again," Sharon said. "This place is beautiful. And it's huge." She walked past Mara. "Look over there. There's a living room and a dining room. Six people can sit here and eat. This is sweet. Talk about upgrade."

"I'm stunned." A smile froze on Mara's face. "Let's go see what your room looks like."

They hurried out of the suite and walked next door. Sharon put her card key in and waited for the green light. She opened the door to a very nice double-bed room, but it was nothing like Mara's.

"I could get jealous," Sharon remarked, "but since you're the one who brought me over here, and since we can open the doors between the rooms, this will do just fine."

"So we'll make sure we tell them we want the doors unlocked." Mara felt extremely generous.

"And look." Sharon walked over to the window. "I've got a great view just like you've got."

"I didn't even look at the view, I was so taken by everything else," Mara replied. "I'm going to go see."

She went out into the hall as the bellboy approached her room.

"Just in time," Mara said. She unlocked the door and walked inside with the bellboy behind her. "You can put my luggage right over there."

He followed her instructions.

"And we would also like . . . My girlfriend is staying in the room you saw me coming out of."

"Yes, ma'am."

"We'd like to unlock that door between my room and hers."

"I will put in that request, ma'am."

"Great." Mara gave him a tip.

"Have you found everything in your room to be okay, ma'am?" The bellboy stood at attention.

"What I've seen is more than okay."

He smiled. "You must know this is one of the best, if not the best, suites we have in the hotel."

Mara beamed. "I can easily believe that."

"And you know how to use your telephone and everything?"

"I believe so." Mara walked over to the telephone on her nightstand. "Oh, there's a light blinking."

"If the light is blinking, ma'am, you must have a message."

Immediately she thought of Jairo. Mara's forehead creased. "I guess I do."

"Do you know how to retrieve it, ma'am?"

"I think I can figure it out," Mara replied.

"Then you have a good day, ma'am. And once I put your friend's luggage in her room, I'll make sure someone comes up and unlocks the door."

"Thanks," Mara said as she looked at the red, blinking light. She tried to remain calm, but she hoped, almost prayed, that it was Jairo.

Mara sat down on the king-size bed. She picked up the receiver and pressed the button that said *messages*. An automated system kicked in, but the flutter in Mara's stomach stopped when she heard an unfamiliar male voice.

"This is Eduardo. This message is for Mara Scott. As a member of the American samba tour, we welcome you to Rio de Janeiro, and we want to invite you to a special dinner being held for your group this evening. It is being held at the Antiquarius. At six." He took a deep breath. "We would love for you to come. Actually, your presence is mandatory." He gave a light laugh. "When you arrive at the restaurant just ask for the special reserved table for the American samba group. The dress is dinner casual. Last but not least, an invitation with the address will be waiting for you at the reception desk downstairs. A taxi can be taken at little cost." He paused. "I look forward to seeing you, and once again, welcome to Rio."

Mara hung up the telephone. For a moment she felt disappointed, but then she looked around. "What's there to be disappointed about? I'm in Rio de Janeiro." She walked into the oversized bathroom with a Jacuzzi tub and steam shower. "I can't wait to tell Sharon what's on our agenda for tonight." She looked in the mirror and struck a

pose. "The Antiquarius. I am going to the Antiquarius in Rio de Janeiro," she repeated, glad that
she had permanently switched to contact lenses.
"And you know what, Mr. Jairo Camara, you can kiss
my grits. It doesn't matter that you didn't think
enough of me to call me again. It doesn't matter at
all. My life is moving forward without you."

There was the sound of applause. "That's right.
You tell him, girl." Sharon stepped into view.

"Oh, no, you heard me." Mara looked at Sharon
through the mirror.

"I heard you all right. And you hear this, Mr.
Camara." Sharon struck a pose beside Mara. "She
doesn't need you or any other man that's half-
stepping in the emotional department. And how
dare you go after my friend like she was just a one-
night stand? But as you can see," she pointed at
Mara, "one monkey don't stop no show."

"Yeah." Mara looked down. "How dare you, Mr.
Camara?" she repeated softly. "How dare you get
my hopes up like that? How dare you present a
dream and simply let it fade away without a word?"
Mara looked into Sharon's eyes through the mirror.

"But that's for real, Mara." Sharon's tone was
somber. "How dare he? But as they say, God don't
like ugly, and here we are enjoying a trip to Rio, at
his expense, and he probably doesn't even know
it."

"That's right. And the party has just begun."
Mara faced Sharon. "There was a phone message
that said we, the American samba tour, are to meet
at a restaurant called the Antiquarius for dinner."

"We just got here and we're already on the go."

Sharon gave her shoulder a lucky brush. "What time does it start?"

"At six o'clock."

"Well, we better start getting ready." Sharon danced out of the bathroom.

Chapter 17

Mara paid the taxi driver and they got out of the car. They entered the restaurant and Mara could see how the the Antiquarius got its name. It was furnished with antique furniture, and collectibles were being sold on the mezzanine level.

"I'd call this an upscale restaurant," Sharon said. "I thought you said we weren't to dress fancy. That it was no big deal."

"That's what the guy said in the phone message." Mara glanced at several of the patrons. They were dressed quite well.

"*Boa noite,*" the maitre d' said. "May I help you?"

"Yes. We are here as a part of the American samba group."

"Welcome." She smiled. "A few of your party are here already. Would you like to come with me?"

She did not wait for an answer, as Mara and Sharon fell in step behind her. They followed her to a table that was set for thirteen, and seven people were already seated. One of them, a short man with a meticulous mustache and twinkling eyes, stood up as they approached.

"*Boa noite,* ladies. Did I have the pleasure of speaking with you on the telephone?"

"No," Mara said. "You left me a message. I'm Mara Scott, and this is my friend Sharon Vegas."

"Yes, I did leave a message for you." He smiled. "Wonderful to meet both of you. My name is Eduardo. I am your coordinator while you are here in Rio. As you can see, several of the winners and their guests are already here. But please," he motioned, "sit wherever you like."

Eduardo returned to his seat, and Mara and Sharon sat down.

"And now it's time for introductions again," Eduardo said. "We've done this before, and I doubt if it will be the last time we do it tonight." He laughed infectiously.

Mara listened as the introductions were made. There were four women and two men, which included two couples. Moments later another couple joined them and introductions were repeated, but Eduardo kept the conversation flowing in a light, friendly manner. Questions about where people were from and how long they had been samba dancing were par for the course.

"Good evening." A waiter interrupted them. "I see there are two empty seats. Are you waiting for more guests?"

"Yes, we are," Eduardo replied. "But we can order drinks. Is that okay?" He looked around.

There was a wave of consents.

"Have you had a chance to look at the drinks on the menu?" Eduardo asked the woman beside him.

"I did, but I don't have a clue what some of them are," she replied honestly.

Eduardo nodded. "Perhaps I can order something for the entire table."

"Sounds good to us." Vivian, a very animated woman from Chicago spoke for everyone. Individual consents followed.

"Bring a selection of *sucos, cervejas,* and *cachaca,*" Eduardo said without hesitation.

"Right away," the waiter replied and walked away.

"So what did you order?" one of the men asked.

"Fruit juices, our favorite beer, and a Brazilian alcoholic drink." Eduardo replied.

"I've heard about the alcohol. It's made from sugarcane," the man replied. "And I'm looking forward to trying it."

"I've got a question," a blonde from Georgia said. "It's about the drawing."

"Go ahead," Eduardo encouraged.

"I know we are the winners of a national drawing, but it's not associated with the dance federation's competitions, is it? Because I know there is a federation."

"Absolutely not," Eduardo said. "It is under the sole jurisdiction of JC's Dance Studio. This contest is held in America, and it is privately operated. If you did not know, the JC stands for Jairo Camara, a master dancer and businessman." Eduardo smiled. "He agreed to hold this contest several years ago, and in general stays abreast of what goes on."

"I've seen a few pictures of him," Vivian said. "He's really handsome. Is he married?"

Mara watched a couple of the ladies nod and laugh.

"No, Mr. Camara is not married," Eduardo replied. "He is quite the eligible bachelor."

"And I bet he's got his pick and enjoys his status," the other male guest said.

Eduardo shrugged. "I only work for him, so who knows? But you can imagine a man of Mr. Camara's status is quite sought after, if I may put it that way, from women of families with money and those who simply are beautiful. And there are so many of you." He smiled and looked around the table.

"Eduardo," Vivian said, "we were told there would be four winners chosen from the North, East, South, and West, but as we sit, there are ten of us here. Does that mean that was not the criteria for the drawing?"

Eduardo cleared his throat. "Basically, that was how it was handled. The drawing was made from each major section of your country to come up with the winners."

"But with a drawing . . ." Vivian looked confused. "Did something happen where there was a tie? Because I think," she pointed at Mara, "you said you were from Florida and didn't you say," she turned to the petite blonde, "you were from Georgia?"

Mara looked at the Georgian. "Yes," she said in unison with the blonde, then continued. "And you competed in Georgia?"

"I sure did, and won the intermediate female singles."

"So did I," Mara said. "And we are both from the South."

They all looked at Eduardo.

"Wait a minute. Wait a minute." He showed everyone his palms. "I see I am going to have to clear this up." Eduardo took out his Palm Pilot and began to search. "I believe there was only one winner from the South."

"But you've got two people sitting here," Vivian said.

"That's true." Eduardo studied the tiny screen. "Here we are. There was one winner from the south, and it was Georgia." He pointed to the blonde. "She was the one who actually won the drawing. And Miss Scott, Mara, may I call you Mara?"

"Yes, you may." Mara's brows were nearly touching.

"I didn't realize you didn't know this, but you were brought here under special circumstances. You are a guest of Mr. Camara's."

"I am?" Mara's mouth dropped.

"You mean Mr. Camara, as in Jairo Camara?" Vivian asked. "The man we were just talking about?"

"Yes," Eduardo replied.

Vivian looked at Mara. "Don't you have friends in high places."

"Evidently." Mara gave Sharon the eye.

"Come on, you can tell us," Vivian said. "You had to know that Mr. Camara had set you and a friend up to come to Brazil and stay."

Mara was beginning to think she didn't like this Vivian very much. "As strange as it sounds, no, I didn't."

"Really?" Vivian looked unconvinced. "Are you going to also tell us you have never met him before?"

"Yes, of course I've met him." Mara went on the

defensive. "I met him in Orlando at JC's Dance Studio, and at the state samba contest." *Although I don't think it's any of your business.*

"Well, obviously you made quite an impression. You say you won the intermediate female singles?"

"I most certainly did," Mara replied.

Vivian winked. "But you never know, with the kind of pull you seem to have."

Several people snickered.

"What are you trying to say? That I didn't win? That it was given to me?"

Vivian shrugged. "I've never seen you dance, but you have to admit your story is a strange one. It's quite impressive, girl." She attempted to lighten the mood.

Mara felt Sharon's knee butt up against hers. She looked at her, but Sharon was looking toward the entrance of the restaurant. Mara looked too. There were Jairo and Gene walking toward the table.

Eduardo stood up immediately. "Mr. Camara, I kept your coming a secret, as you suggested." His smile broadened, if that was possible. "But the conversation took a turn such that I thought I might have to tell them. You arrived right on time."

Jairo smiled. *"Boa noite."* He looked around the table and his gaze rested on Mara. "Mara."

He was thinner than Mara remembered, which added a sharpness to his good looks that made him photo-ready for any magazine. "Hello," she replied, stunned to see him again.

"Boa noite, Sharon."

"Hi." Sharon waved.

"We've ordered plenty of drinks for the table," Eduardo said, "to get the ball rolling."

Jairo and Gene took a seat at the end of the table near Mara and Sharon.

"I'm sure you've been an excellent host, as usual, Eduardo." Jairo leaned back in his chair. "I want to welcome all of you to my city. To Rio de Janeiro. It's obvious your efforts in the American samba contests have paid off. You are the lucky winners of the national drawing, and we have a couple of things for you to do while you are here. But by far the majority of the time is yours. Please feel free to pursue whatever your interests may be." He looked around the table. "But there will be a dance tomorrow night. I hope you will all come."

"Mr. Camara." Vivian leaned on the table. "I just want to say it's a pleasure meeting you. I have heard so much about you, and I'm truly honored that you would take the time out and come to this."

"The pleasure is all mine." Jairo looked at Mara, then around the table. "I'm sure."

"How long have you been dancing, Mr. Camara?" another guest asked.

"Many, many years," Jairo replied. "I love the dance. The samba. And it has been good to me, and therefore as a result I decided to start JC's Dance Studio in America."

Mara stayed quiet as the conversation progressed. It was almost more than she could take in. Jairo was responsible for her and Sharon being in Rio. She had not won the drawing, and now he sat only a few feet away from her, acting as if he had done nothing out of the ordinary. As if buying tickets for people to Brazil was no more than buying an evening's dinner. *And for a man with his money, it probably equates to just that.* Mara thought. *Jairo probably feels he can do whatever he wants, whenever he wants, to whomever he wants. I bet people like me are props in his play.*

Except for the initial hello, Jairo hadn't said a word to her, and considering how Mara discovered the origins of her trip to Rio, she was more than a little uncomfortable. Mara was certain the others were aware of Jairo's silence, too, and she could feel their eyes on her, especially Vivian. Eduardo was no exception.

The drinks were brought to the table and choices were made.

"Is this the *cachaca*?" The man who had inquired about it earlier pointed at a frosted glass.

"Yes, it is," Jairo replied.

"Good." He pulled it toward him. "I can't wait to taste this because I've heard so much about it."

"Then you know it is made from sugarcane," Jairo said.

"I sure do."

"And also,"—Jairo leaned toward the man. It brought him conveniently closer to Mara—"let me tell you a secret. The best *cachaca* is always made on the Brazilian farms. There on the small farms it," he made a movement with his hand, "is superb. But I'm sure you will enjoy this one as well." Jairo sat back.

The conversation continued with no private words between Jairo and Mara, and Mara didn't feel it was her duty to initiate them. Eventually food was ordered. It included *perna de carneiro* (leg

of lamb), codfish that was stewed in coconut sauce
and tomato, and a soup of palm hearts (*crème de
palmito*). Dessert was also placed on the table—a
chocolate ball made of condensed milk and cocoa
called *brigadeiro*.

But by then Mara felt as if someone had dunked
her in a pool and told her to hold her breath. Her
mind was full and her body jittery. She was beginning to resent Jairo's silence. Everyone knew that
he had paid her way there for his own private reasons, and for Jairo not to show their connection
made Mara feel, and she was sure the others thought
it, that the relationship was not worthy of attention,
that it was a relationship that was only to be con-
ducted behind closed doors. *I've come all the way to
Rio to gain this kind of reputation?* Mara had never
been in this position and didn't quite know what
to do about it. Just as she was mulling it over, Jairo
looked at her.

"So how have you been, Mara Scott? It is good to
see you here in Rio."

"With this unexpected turn of events, things
have turned a little strange, but up till then I was
enjoying it," she replied. Mara saw a special spark
in Jairo's eyes, but he kept the conversation on an
even keel.

"And all of your accommodations, your ride
from the airport, and your hotel room have been
good?"

He's too suave to take that bait. "Very good," Mara
replied. "Very good indeed."

"Excellent," Jairo said. "I want your stay here to
be enjoyable." He looked around the table. "And
that goes for the rest of you. I want you to enjoy
Brazil and have a memorable experience in Rio."

Dinner continued, but that was the extent of their exchange. Jairo was constantly being asked questions and engaged in some conversation or other. All the while Mara kept thinking he would say more to her, at least explain why he had sent for her, but Jairo never did.

Finally, Mara had enough. She couldn't wait to finish her meal so that she could leave. Somehow knowing that she was an impostor of sorts, had been brought to Rio for less than official reasons with everyone knowing it, was difficult for Mara to take. No sooner than she took a couple of mouthfuls of the chocolate, she turned to Sharon. "I'm ready to go. How about you?"

Sharon looked down at her half-eaten *brigadeiro*, then back at Mara. "If you are, I guess so."

"I am." Mara said emphatically. "I'm not feeling very well."

"No." Sharon looked as if she was trying to ascertain if Mara was telling the truth or not.

"Of course you can stay if you like."

Sharon visibly relaxed. "All right. Maybe I'll stay a little longer and finish this." She put another spoonful of the chocolate in her mouth.

Mara kicked her under the table.

Sharon jerked. "But on second thought, if you're feeling really, really bad I guess I should go with you."

Mara's eyes bore into Sharon. "I'm feeling very bad." She pushed her chair away from the table. Sharon did the same.

Jairo looked at Mara. "Excuse me." He interrupted his conversation with another diner. "Are you leaving already?"

"Yes, I don't feel very well." She gave him a challenging look. "So I need to go. But please, don't stop because of me." Mara looked at the other guests. Vivian was covering a smile with her hand.

Eduardo came over and stood beside her. "Sorry you're not feeling well." He sounded sincere. "I'll call you and give you the details about the dance. If you're not in your room, I'll leave a message like I did before." He patted her upper arm gently. "Hope you feel better soon. Perhaps it was our Brazilian food. It can be a little heavy for people who are not accustomed to eating like this."

"I hope I feel better too," Mara replied. She looked around the table. "And I'll see you all at the dance."

Chapter 18

"I can't believe it. I can't believe it," Mara said between her teeth as they walked through the restaurant.

"Calm down now. Everybody's going to hear you," Sharon said.

"If I don't get out of here in a minute, I'm going to scream," Mara warned.

"All right." Sharon smiled at a woman who gave them a suspicious glance. "Just a few more steps, Mara, and we'll be out of here."

Finally, Mara pushed the door open and they walked out onto the sidewalk. But Mara kept walking and Sharon tried to keep up with her. Suddenly, Mara stopped, turned, and looked at Sharon.

"What is happening here? This can't be real. It's like a nightmare."

"Well-l." Sharon bent forward a bit. "It's all according to how you want to look at it. You are here in Rio, and the bills have been paid. Jairo was aware of what was going on all along . . ." She turned up one palm. "You thought he didn't know," she turned up the other, "but now you know he did. It's really not that big a difference."

"I could look at it that way." Mara nodded for a second, then her teeth gritted again. "Or I could look at it like everybody sitting at that table, besides Jairo, who knows the truth, thinks that I'm Jairo's lay of the week. Maybe lay of the day." Mara's eyes widened. "What about lay of the night? One of the three would probably apply."

"Mara, you are so old fashioned."

"No." Mara wagged her finger. "My mother taught me 'reputation is everything.' "

"But hey, we know what your situation is with Jairo," Sharon said.

"Yeah, we know," Mara replied. "You and I, but what about everybody else?"

"Well, who cares about everybody else? We don't know those people. We'll probably see them at the dance, but then when will you see them again?"

Mara put her hand to her forehead. "That's true." She exhaled.

Sharon's brows rose. "But you'll probably see them at some of the competitions if you keep dancing, and you better." She pointed at Mara. "You're good enough. With time you could beat them all."

Now both hands went up to Mara's forehead. "Well thanks a lot, Sharon, for reminding me that I could possibly gain a reputation on the dance circuit as the woman who wins using something other than her feet."

"Now, see, if you were somebody else, I'd think you might be joking, but I know you really mean it." Sharon folded her arms. "From the way that Vivian was looking at Jairo, I bet she wished she were in your shoes."

"Well I don't." Mara closed her eyes. "Now I really feel sick to my stomach."

"Aw-w it's just the excitement of seeing Jairo again. You thought you had him behind you. You were getting your strength back." Sharon took Mara's arm.

"And you know what's even worse?"

"What?"

"Jairo didn't make it any better. He barely talked to me, let alone initiated a conversation that would have made it plain to everyone that we only got together for one evening. And nothing happened." She looked at Sharon. "No, what was he doing? Listening and talking to everybody but me." Mara shook her head. "What time is it?"

Sharon looked at her watch. "It's almost eight o'clock."

"It's too early to go back to the hotel." Mara pouted.

Sharon stopped walking. "My thought exactly. I've got a suggestion."

"What's that?" Mara looked defeated.

"We can always go shopping at that mall I told you I read about."

"What mall?"

"Rio Sul. I read it's open until ten at night and they have four hundred shops. What better way to take your mind away from all of this than designer shops and jewelry stores at Brazilian prices?" Sharon smiled enticingly.

"I don't know if I'm in the mood for all that."

"Come on, Mara. Look at you." Sharon stepped

back. "You look like a wet noodle. Have some heart. Life could be much worse, you know, than being able to go shopping in Rio de Janeiro."

"That's true." Mara surrendered. "All right, you've talked me into it."

They hailed a cab, and in minutes they were at Rio Sul, and for at least an hour and a half Mara chewed Sharon's ear about Jairo. Still, by the time the shopping was over and they were in a cab, exhausted, Mara hadn't had enough.

"You know, he looked much thinner than I remembered."

"Who?" Sharon rested her head against the back seat.

"Jairo, of course."

"Of course." Sharon shook her head. "Who else?"

"He did," Mara said. "He was much thinner."

Sharon opened one eye. "I think we've spoken about this before. You've said a lot, but I'm quite sure we've already covered this."

"But he was." Mara bit her lip. "I know he was."

"I don't remember, but please forgive me for not being as fixated on Jairo Camara as you are."

Mara looked at Sharon. "Fixated."

"Yes." Sharon opened both eyes. "Fixated. Do you realize you've been talking about him nonstop for as long as we were shopping?"

"I can't help it if this is a bizarre situation," Mara defended herself. "I mean, what's going on here?"

"I know." Sharon closed her eyes again. "And believe me I sympathize with you. And Lord knows how many women would just be devastated that a gorgeous man, a trillionaire maybe," she exaggerated, "has secretly flown them and a friend to Rio de Janeiro. Just because he wants to see her."

Mara sat quietly. "But it's not that simple." Her voice went soft.

"Maybe it isn't. But you can't argue that what I said is basically true." Sharon nudged Mara with her elbow. "You didn't come up with this in one of your daydreams, did you?"

"Not in a million years," Mara replied.

The cab stopped in front of the Golden Tulip. They paid the driver and went up the elevator.

"That shopping has worn me out. Suddenly I'm so tired," Sharon said. "I'm sure jetlag isn't helping. I'm going to go to my room, take a bath, and crash."

"Me too," Mara replied softly.

"You'll be all right. Just count your blessings," Sharon reminded her.

"I'll try to do that." Mara took a couple of steps toward her room. "Sharon."

"Un-huh."

"Do you think it's possible that I didn't really win the contest? That it was faked by Jairo?"

"Why would he do that?" Sharon asked.

Mara walked back toward her. "Maybe it's like they said."

"I don't remember what they said. What? That you were so irresistible, that you were such a desirable woman that he rigged the entire contest just to give you a prize and have you ride around in his limousine?" She looked skeptical. "He could have just invited you to party with him in the limo without the prize."

"Yeah, I guess so."

"Think. You're a smart woman. It's not 'I guess so,'" Sharon argued. "It doesn't make any sense, Mara. Stop second-guessing yourself. You've always had that problem. You try to make sure things are perfect, always according to the rules, because with all your schooling and brains, there's a part of you that still doesn't believe in yourself. Stop doing it. It's not doing you any good."

Mara's eyes confirmed that what Sharon said was true. "It's because I've always had this fanciful part of me that dreams. Boy, can I dream. And I have to fight to make sure I'm not mixing those dreams up with reality." She hoped Sharon understood. "I really am a dreamer, Sharon. I'm so comfortable there, and I only took the traditional path because my mother wanted me to. Now, I use that creativity to help others dream up projects." Mara sighed. "But sometimes your girlfriend walks a very fine line."

"Oh-h." Sharon hugged her. "It's dreamers like you that hold this world accountable. You want the fairytale, and it makes the rest of us want it too."

Mara smiled. "Good night."

"Good night." Sharon walked up the hall.

Chapter 19

Deep in thought, Mara entered her hotel room. She walked over to the telephone, but there was no blinking light. She hated that she was disappointed. Mara dropped her shopping bags on the floor and headed straight to the bathroom, where she soaked in the tub. Although she tried to relax in the hot, sudsy water, the restaurant scene played in her head over and over again. Mara couldn't get the image of Jairo's face out of her mind.

Mara got out of the tub, put on her robe, sat on the side of her bed, and put on the hotel's lotion. It was exceptionally nice. She concentrated on her elbows and her feet.

The telephone rang. Mara picked the receiver up so fast, she nearly dropped it. "Hello."

"Ms. Scott, this is the reception desk."

Her eyes rolled toward the ceiling. "Yes."

"You have a delivery. Can it be brought up?"

"A delivery, at this hour?"

"Yes, ma'am. We have some beautiful flowers here for you."

Jairo. Mara brightened. "Well . . . Sure you can bring them up."

"Thank you, ma'am."

She hung up as a smile spread across her face. This time she knew the flowers were from Jairo, and she felt instant happiness. Mara picked up the telephone to let Sharon know, but then she hung up. "She's been so patient with me. I've already talked her head off about this man. I think I'll let her rest."

Moments later the doorbell rang. Mara looked through the viewer and saw a bouquet of flowers. She opened the door immediately. There stood Jairo with the flowers in his hand.

"Hello." His voice was deep. "These are for you."

Their eyes locked.

"Thank you," Mara said.

"Aren't you going to take them and invite me in?" His raven dark head tilted to the side.

She reached out her hand. "I will take the flowers, but—"

"Please, Mara. No buts. I have gone through so much trouble to bring you here to Rio. Many clandestine operations." His eyes softened. "Can you not invite me in for a moment?"

Mara held the bouquet in her hand. She burned to let him know what had been said at the Antiquarius before he arrived, and how she felt about what people were, most likely, thinking of her. But when she looked into his eyes again, all Mara could say was, "Sure. Come in."

She walked into the suite and placed the flowers

on the dining table as Jairo closed the door. Mara stared at them. It was the most beautiful bouquet she had ever received. She looked at Jairo. "They're lovely."

"I'm glad you like them." He stood with his hands in his pockets. "Do you like the room as well?"

Mara looked around. "You mean my having the master suite was not a mistake?"

Jairo chuckled. "No, it was no mistake." He took a couple of steps forward. "You see, my friend is one of the owners of the Golden Tulip. Sometimes we call one another and ask for favors." His dark eyes twinkled.

"This is unreal." Mara shook her head. "If it wasn't happening to me, I simply would not believe it."

"Would not believe what?"

"That you would go through so much, just for me."

"Attraction and love have no rules, Mara. At least I don't know of any. Do you?"

She looked down. "No, I don't."

"And for me it is as simple as that."

"Yeah I guess it is," Mara's chin lifted, "when you have as much money as you have. You are able to do whatever you want. Have whatever you want." She stared at him. "It is as simple as that."

"Forgive me." Jairo sat down without being asked. "But I am very tired, and if you're going to bring my money up this quickly, I must sit down."

Mara remained standing.

Jairo rubbed his eyes. "Yes, I can do many things. My money opens many doors for me, Mara. But money cannot open every door. And after a while a man needs to know if it is him or his money that a woman wants. Granted, sometimes it is both." Jairo paused. "And I figured, after you did not try to track me down, it wasn't my money you were after. If it was, you would have been much more aggressive."

Their eyes locked again.

Mara looked away. "Is that how it works?" She trembled as she sat on the couch. "I guess even the wealthy have their problems."

"Yes, even the wealthy have limitations," Jairo replied.

Silence filled the suite again.

"So have you truly been enjoying Rio?" He went to safer ground.

"Oh, it's an amazing city," Mara replied. "Really amazing."

"So you do . . . like it?" The question had more than one connotation.

Mara licked her lips. "Yes, Jairo. I like it. I like it a lot."

They shared a tiny smile.

Mara felt even more nervous. "Of course, I haven't done much traveling, none at all to tell the truth, and it may be that I am quite easily impressed. Unlike you." Her gaze softened as she looked at him, and Mara tried to hide it by looking away. "You do it all the time. So I guess when you come to a city like Orlando, Florida, it's nothing special for you." Their eyes held again. "It's just the same old hat."

"That's not true." Jairo's eyes roamed her face. "I can appreciate each place for what it is. Every place has its own uniqueness. It does not have to be a Rio, a Paris, or Rome. And Orlando has its landmark. Disney World."

Mara laughed. "Yeah, we do have Disney World." Then her expression turned serious. "But I guess not even Disney World was enough to remind you to call me as you promised." She looked down. "Not enough."

"No, Disney World was not enough," Jairo replied. "But knowing you were there, Mara, was."

She clicked her tongue several times. "Don't go too far, Jairo. Don't tell me things that aren't true. I'm already leery enough. I'm sitting on the edge of skepticism and it's mighty sharp."

"There's no need to be there, Mara. It's such an uncomfortable place." He paused. "I thought of you. Did you not think of me?"

Mara exhaled. "We're not talking about what I thought of. I'm not the globetrotter, and I'm not the one who promised he would call."

"That is true." Jairo rubbed his hands together as he watched her. "Well the truth is," he rose from his chair and sat beside her on the couch, "I thought of you an awful lot." His dark eyes searched her face. "But I was in no position to call you."

"And why was that?" She could not bring herself to look at him while he sat so close.

"Because, Mara, I've been very ill. Very ill indeed."

Surprised, she looked at his face. "You've been sick?"

"I have. Very sick, Mara. I was even in the hospital for a while."

"Oh no." Her eyes filled with concern. "What was wrong?"

"I had walking pneumonia, and being the man that I am, I refused to acknowledge how bad I was feeling until the doctor told me, if my body had not given up on me as it did, we may never have sat like this again."

"Oh no," Mara repeated.

"And that is what I said to myself while I was in the hospital," Jairo replied. "'Oh no.' Those days lying in bed so weak I could not walk. During that time your mind thinks of all kinds of bad things. But you definitely think of the good things, too, the things that you would cherish and do, if you got the chance. And one of the things that came to me was, I would definitely want to see Mara Scott again. I would definitely make it happen, no matter what." He touched her hand. "But then I would think, but we left under such a harsh note, so unpleasant, and I didn't think an ordinary call could make up for that. And from how you spoke to me, I didn't think that you would have accepted an invitation to my country if I had extended it to you. So, as stupid as it sounds, I hoped with all of my heart, that you would win the drawing, but when you didn't I pulled some strings to include you in the trip." He smiled like a kid who knew he'd done something wrong. That made Mara smile too. His eyes softened and he touched her face. "But I knew I had to see you again. And I didn't want it to be an evening where you had to run back to work. I wanted to spend time with you so I could get to know you a little better, and you could get to know me."

Mara's eyes were transfixed on Jairo's. They were so close, so dark.

"I noticed that you are thinner," she managed to say.

"Thinner, but fine now. Give me a couple of

weeks, and I'll be back to my normal self." He leaned away from her. "But you say that with such conviction. Do you no longer find me attractive?"

Her gaze softened. "Even more so because of what you've told me."

"Well, if that is true, let me tell you something else." Jairo picked Mara's hands up and kissed them gently. "While I was sick, Mara, I thought of many things. But over and over again I thought of that one evening that we spent together in the limo. I had not had so much fun, ordinary fun, with anyone in a long time. I can't even remember how long. Your heart was open and I could feel your sincere joy. For me," he looked down, "that was such a treasure. You can imagine, I am with so many people, so often, and most of the time I think they all want something from me. Generally, they are not with me because they like me, or think I am a good human being."

Mara nodded. "I can believe that."

"And I didn't sense that from you. And to not recognize you that next day, I'm sorry. I didn't expect to see you in that environment, and the truth is, the night before you did look very different."

"I'm sure I did. I was in costume as a Brazilian samba dancer with lots of makeup and a totally different style of dress, but I still, I would have thought . . ." Mara's voice trailed away.

"You thought that considering the time we had spent together that I would have recognized you. Believe me, I thought the same thing. That's why I was so embarrassed by it all." Jairo paused. "And I knew the anger that you expressed in the hallway covered a lot of hurt."

"I wouldn't say it was hurt." Mara still couldn't admit it. "Disappointment, yes. I couldn't say it was hurt because we hadn't shared enough for that."

He stroked her hand. "We had one night of fun together, and I think there was something special beneath it all. And I really didn't have time to acknowledge it until I was laid up in that bed. Did you feel it?"

"Feel what?" Mara could feel her heart beating.

"The connection that was there?"

Mara hesitated. "To be honest, I-I felt something. But when you didn't call . . ." She shrugged.

"So our one night together did merit your being hurt," Jairo said softly.

Chapter 20

The room became silent again.

Jairo continued. "I hope that bringing you here to Rio under these circumstances will make amends for such an unforgivable oversight. And since I am scheduled to be here until you leave, I hope, despite my business schedule, we can still spend some time together."

Mara felt as if she would drown in his eyes. "I'd like that."

"Now," Jairo pulled her to him, "come to me. Let me hug you. I want to feel you, Mara." He spoke his actions. "Let me lay my head against your hair. I am glad that you are here. You are a special woman. I hope you know that. Any woman who could dance the samba in her own unique way, like you did, and transform into a businesswoman of such professionalism is special in her own right. But you are also special because of what I believe your heart is capable of."

Mara allowed Jairo to hold her. She laid her head

against his shoulder and they stayed like that for an indeterminable amount of time. Then Jairo began to softly squeeze her body. Squeeze and let go, until the motion turned into passionate caresses that made Mara tremble. She tried to control it but it wouldn't stop.

Jairo pulled back, just a bit. "Look at you. Your body is shivering. That is because you respond so fully." He touched his lips to hers in a soft, melting kiss. "So responsive." He rubbed his lips gently against hers. "I can feel you, Mara. There is so much love inside of you just waiting to be given, and there is also desire." He kissed her again; this time it was much deeper. Their lips fused and their tongues explored.

"You taste good," Jairo said seconds later in her ear as he stroked her face, "and I like the way you feel. I remembered the velvety feel of your skin while I lay there." He grazed her neck and went inside her robe, where Jairo began to massage her shoulder. "Your softness would not leave me. And there was a gentleness in your spirit. I wanted some of it. My life has been full of many other things. Some of them no one in their right mind would want, but others . . . many would love to have."

Jairo rubbed the back of Mara's neck and she relaxed against his hand. Then he kissed her again, and his kisses trailed to her ear and down to her chin. He nipped her chin with his teeth before he continued down her exposed throat. Mara allowed Jairo to do what he wanted, and what her mounting desire called out for.

Mara sizzled with each wet, feathery kiss as he created a path of hot and cool. Hot and cool. Hot with the touch of his mouth, cool with the sheen his lips left behind.

"Oh, Mara," Jairo whispered when her robe loosened naturally, and nearly exposed her breasts. "I must see you." He opened the robe further and simply stared for an unending moment before he looked into her eyes. "You are beautiful. So beautiful," he repeated as his eyes remained locked on hers, and he cupped her breast. "So beautiful." He massaged her breasts gently before his head descended and his warm, moist mouth encased her nipple.

Mara closed her eyes and gave in to the moment. Gingerly, she touched his hair before she ran her fingers through it. It was heavier and coarser than she imagined. Then Mara stroked Jairo's face before her arm went around him and pulled him close. Encouraged, Jairo kissed Mara again, and a fire raged between them.

"Mara, will you let me make love to you?" he asked in a husky voice.

She swallowed hard as she felt her body burn, but Mara did not answer. Jairo responded by burying his face between her breasts. Afterward he looked up at her, with a lock of hair nearly in his eye. "Will you let me love you, Mara?"

Her head nodded yes before she could say the word, and Jairo showed his appreciation with a soft kiss. "Then come." He pulled her off the couch, "We must do it right." Jairo led Mara to the king-sized bed, where he pulled back the covers. "Lie here."

Mara watched Jairo remove a condom from his wallet and put it on the bedside before he removed his clothes, and she saw what lay underneath . . .

lean muscles carved under rich, even-toned vanilla skin, with just enough silky hair that met like a flowing river right down the center of his chest to his navel. But when Jairo removed his pants, and Mara saw him, her breath caught in her throat.

He stood before her with his legs spread, and when Mara looked into his eyes there was pure desire. Jairo continued to let Mara take in with her eyes what she would soon take into herself.

"Do you like what you see?"

She covered her heart with her hand. "Jairo, you are magnificent," she whispered.

"What you see is what you bring out in me, Mara." He put on the condom. "What I am now is nothing but desire for you."

Jairo placed one knee on the bed and untied Mara's robe. She sat up so that she could remove the robe from her shoulders, but Jairo kissed her, and Mara forgot about the robe that eventually became a part of the linens. Mara's arms went around Jairo's back and she pulled him down with her. They kissed over and over again, and their bodies rocked and rubbed together.

"I thought about this moment," he said in her ear. "I'd be a liar if I said I hadn't visualized this exact moment, because I want you, Mara. I wanted you that evening, and I want you now." He looked into her eyes. "Do you want me?"

"I do," she replied with her body on fire. Mara knew she had never wanted a man so much. She wanted Jairo so badly, Mara felt as if she might faint.

At that moment Jairo positioned his body slightly to the side of her, and his hands touched her breasts, then ventured downward. When Jairo discovered the moist triangle between her legs, he began to stroke her core before his finger slipped inside and Mara moaned at his mastery. He watched her face as he pleasured her, nearly bringing Mara to orgasm. Jairo held her at that point.

"Are you ready for me, Mara?"

She turned her head from side to side. "Oh, you're torturing me."

Jairo captured her mouth with his own, and went inside with one smooth movement. Their bodies trembled.

"Mara," Jairo called her name. "You are wonderful. Being inside you is just like I imagined." He sucked air through his teeth. "No . . . you are more. You are so much more."

Jairo began to thrust and Mara held on to him. It was mere seconds before Mara was solely aware of the ache that began to build inside of her, and with each stroke of Jairo's body it increased until it filled her mind, her body, and her very being. Then Mara could take it no longer. "Jairo. Jairo. You are—" a moan forced its way out of her just as his mouth descended on hers again in an all-encompassing kiss, and his body quaked.

Chapter 21

"Good morning! Wake up. Wake up," Sharon said as she came through the adjoining door. "I hope you slept well last night, because I did, and I'm ready to get—" She stopped when she saw Jairo and Mara lying entangled in each other's arms. "Oops. My bad." Sharon took a couple of steps back, turned, and walked away.

With sleepy eyes Mara looked at Jairo. He smiled at her.

"Now Sharon knows what you were doing last night instead of sleeping."

Mara smiled again. "And I wasn't doing it alone."

"No," Jairo replied. "You could never do something that good alone." He kissed her. "But what time is it?"

Mara pointed toward the clock. Jairo looked at it, sat up, yawned, and stretched. "I've got to get going. I'm sure I've already missed a couple of phone calls."

Mara turned on her side. "The busy business-man."

"That's me. I've got a meeting this morning, and I've got another one in a couple of hours after that." He swung his feet to the floor, then put on his watch.

"So your day is pretty full." Mara sat up, although she wished they could have made love again.

"Yes, and I can tell you're disappointed." Jairo leaned across the bed and touched her face. "But I hope last night will hold you." A devilish glint entered his eyes. "It was quite a marathon, wouldn't you say?"

Mara's head went back as she laughed. "Oh, yes, it was."

Their gazes locked and held.

"But I've got to go," Jairo apologized.

"I know." Mara pushed him gently so he would continue to dress. "So what will you do? Go home, take a shower, and put on fresh clothes? Or do you have a shower at your office?"

He glanced at her. "Not this one. No, I'll go home." Jairo put on his pants.

"Do you live in Rio?" Mara pulled her knees up to her chest.

"Yes, I have a home very close to the city."

Mara squinted. "I bet it's huge."

Jairo smiled a little. "People have described it in such a way."

In silence, Mara watched him button his shirt. Secretly, she wanted Jairo to invite her to his home, but he did not.

He looked at Mara. "When I think about it, the

entire day is going to be crazy, but tonight is the dance; we'll see each other there."

Mara nodded. *He'll see me there, but he didn't offer to take me.*

"Good. I don't want to be away from you for too long while you're here in Rio." He smiled at her. "Now stand up, naked woman, so I can kiss you before I go."

Mara got up, but she covered herself with the sheet.

"Modesty is alive and well during the day," Jairo said as he watched her come around the bed.

"You could say that," Mara said.

"But I like the day, because in the daylight I can see things much clearer." He attempted to jerk the sheet away, but Mara held fast. Jairo laughed, kissed her, and left.

Mara remained in the middle of the floor holding the sheet. She sighed, then smiled as she remembered their night of love. The sounds. The smells. The feeling. Mara picked up her robe, and with the sheet still draped about her, she entered the bathroom and took a long, hot shower. When Mara emerged from the bathroom, Sharon was sitting in the cushy armchair.

"I thought you'd never come out of there. What were you trying to do? Drown yourself?"

Mara looked at Sharon and shook her head. "No. And my God, didn't you see enough after you walked into my room earlier today? I would think you'd give me a little more privacy."

"You had enough privacy. I sat in that room listening to you shower until I just couldn't take it anymore."

"Your nosiness just couldn't take it anymore."

Mara gave her a look. "I could have been shower-ing with Jairo."

"No, I heard him say he had to go."

Mara put her hand on her hip. "What were you doing, hiding over there?"

"Of course not." Sharon's chin lifted. "Just walk-ing slowly."

"You are too nosy," Mara replied.

"Do you blame me? I come in here all bright-eyed and bushy-tailed thinking, okay, Mara and I are going to hit the streets of Rio. I walk in here full of verve, and there's a man in your bed. Not any man, of course, but Jairo Camara."

"Well, I guess the next time you'll knock before you come in," Mara said smiling.

"Don't you shift the blame on me. What was Jairo doing in here? How did that come about?"

"He gave me some flowers. And he delivered them himself."

"He sure did deliver himself." Sharon smiled too. She leaned forward. "How was it?"

Mara made a face. "None of your business."

"Aw-w come on, now. You've got to tell me."

"Look, what happens in my bed and in my bed-room is none of your business. You never asked about James, and I've certainly never asked you about Roberto."

"Okay. All right." Sharon sat back. "But neither one of them is JC." She made a movement like a bodybuilder. "So I figure it either was really good or really bad. Because you either were trying to drown yourself in that shower, or you were so wrapped up in the memory that you didn't realize you were in there for thirty minutes."

Mara exhaled. "Let's chalk it up to the memories."

"I knew it. I knew it." Sharon slapped her knee. "You look like you've died and gone to heaven. Look at you. You're shining like a flashlight."

Mara laughed again. "Stop. Stop. You're so busy trying to get into my business that you aren't even dressed." She pointed at Sharon's robe.

"Now that I know what I know," Sharon smiled, "we can move on. Are you hungry?"

"I could eat anything you put in front of me," Mara replied.

"I bet you could, you little hussy you. All right. I'm going to get dressed. You do the same, and let's go and have a heavy Portuguese breakfast."

Mara laughed again when Sharon left the room.

Chapter 22

Later that evening

"Look at this." Sharon looked inside the ballroom. "This place is something else. And look how large it is."

"I'm impressed." Mara looked too.

"I thought this was going to be a little dance for . . . I don't know, us. For you all, at least." Sharon watched a constant flow of people go into the ballroom.

"I was operating under that premise as well," Mara replied.

"Didn't Jairo give you any hints last night?"

"No," Mara said. "We didn't talk about dancing."

"Yeah, I guess you didn't." Sharon grinned. She crooked her neck. "And look at some of these people. They are dressed to the nines."

"They sure are." She thought about her night

with Jairo. "But wait a minute. We're not doing too bad."

"You're right," Sharon replied. "I've got on my favorite dress, and it's shocking red. So this Puerto Rican woman can stand up against any of these Brazilian beauties." She nudged Mara. "Me in my red and you in your purple. Sweet. Real sweet. We're going to give them something to talk about." She pulled Mara's off-the-shoulder dress down a little further. "There, that's for good measure."

"Are we ready?" Mara asked.

"We are ready," Sharon replied. "And we're going to dance tonight. Show these folks that the African roots running through all our cultures are strong. We know how to shake a tail feather too." Sharon tugged at Mara's hand and they entered the ballroom. Mara and Sharon walked through the door and stopped a few yards away from the entrance. There were at least fifty round tables in the room, and a large dance floor split the room in half. The room was more than half filled with people laughing, drinking, and dancing. Mara noticed a long table with a variety of foods at the back of the room. She also noticed a large crowd of people gathered to the right of it. Sharon noticed them too.

"I wonder what's going on over there?"

"I don't know," Mara replied, just as a burst of laughter erupted from the group.

"Boa noite." Eduardo popped up beside them as a Brazilian tune kicked off. "I'm glad you could make it. How are you feeling tonight, Mara?"

For a second Mara looked confused; then she remembered her excuse from the night before. "I feel fine," she replied. "I'm my old self again."

"Great, because we want everyone to enjoy themselves tonight." His eyes roamed the room. "So enjoy the food," he motioned, "the drinks, and by all means enjoy some dancing." He smiled and kept moving before Mara or Sharon could say another word.

It was obvious this was not a crowd that needed to be coaxed into dancing, as large numbers of people headed toward the dance floor. The majority of the women were dressed in colorful form-fitted dresses, and Mara thought she had never seen so many men with open shirts on one dance floor. But she was also struck by their physical beauty. Mara and Sharon watched a couple right in front of them begin to dance, and could they dance. "Oh, my goodness. Look at them go," Mara said. They both stared. "It's like it's in their blood."

"I'm telling you," Sharon replied. "I said we were going to show them a thing or two, but honey, I don't know, because these natives can do the samba."

Mara continued to watch people dance until the crowd that had caught their attention earlier parted. Mara looked. In the center was Jairo laughing, and as if they were on cue, the rest of the crowd laughed whenever Jairo laughed. One of the women slipped her arm around Jairo's waist and kissed his cheek. Jairo kissed her on her cheek and Mara looked back at the dance floor.

"Look at that couple in the banana yellow go." Sharon was still focused on the dancers.

"Yeah," Mara replied.

Sharon looked at her. "What's wrong?"

"I said yeah, look at them."

"I know, but you sound like you've just lost your best friend."

Mara continued to watch the dancers. "Although it's early, I think I've already had more entertainment than I expected."

"Say what?" Sharon squinted.

Mara motioned with her head.

Sharon looked. "Oh-h-h. Jairo's over there. Come on, let's go say hello."

"No." Mara held her back.

"Why not?" Sharon asked. "If anybody has the right to, you do. You earned it last night." She grinned.

But Mara's expression was serious. "I'm not kidding, Sharon. We are not going over there."

"All right." Sharon backed down. "It's definitely your call, although I don't see why not."

"Because . . ." Mara couldn't bring herself to say what she was thinking. "He's busy."

Sharon shrugged. "Okay. We'll wait."

Sharon continued to look in Jairo's direction. Mara pretended the dance floor was her focus, but out of the corner of her eye she could see everything. She saw a man slap Jairo on the back. Jairo smiled a smile that nearly melted her heart, and the same woman that kissed him on the cheek, slipped her hand in his and whispered in Jairo's ear. Now Mara could no longer pretend she wasn't interested, and she and Sharon watched. The woman began to walk away, but Jairo reached out as if to stop her. He shook his head no, but she touched his face as if she knew it very well, placed one finger on his lips, then walked away again. To Mara, Jairo looked displeased, but he seemed to forget within seconds as he focused on the people around him.

"Now I see why," Sharon said.

Mara just looked at her.

"But who knows, maybe she's his cousin."

"Do you have a cousin who acts like that?"

"No. But we're in Rio, things could be different," Sharon replied.

"I don't think so," Mara said as she watched the woman cross the dance floor dressed in a magnificent burnt orange dress that fitted every curve down to a circle of ruffles above her knees.

"Have you ever seen anybody twist their hips that much when they walk?" Sharon rolled her eyes. "That makes no sense. No sense at all."

Mara blew lightly. "Her walk is the samba."

"I wonder who she is?"

"Who knows," Mara replied. "But she's obviously someone who knows Jairo. And knows him well." She looked down. "I can't believe the next day after I've made love to the man, I get to see my competition. And from where I stand," she looked down at herself, "the competition is really tough."

Mara and Sharon continued to watch the woman as she approached the bandstand.

"There's Eduardo." Sharon pointed as Eduardo showed all thirty-two teeth when the woman spoke to him. At the end of their conversation he nearly bowed in front of the bandstand stairs. "My goodness, is she royalty or something?" Sharon remarked.

But Mara kept silent as she watched the drama continue to unfold. The woman mounted the bandstand steps and spoke to a man that was obviously connected, by his style of dress, to the musicians, although he was not playing.

"I hate to say it," Sharon said, "but that is some dress she is wearing."

"Well, don't say it," Mara retorted, then glanced at Jairo. He was in his own world.

Mara looked back at the woman. She chatted with the man until the music was over. Afterward he said something to the musicians, and the woman walked up to the microphone. She began to speak in Portuguese. Her gestures were graceful as she spoke and smiled.

"I wish I knew what she was saying," Mara whispered.

"Me too." Sharon looked around.

Then the woman said Jairo's name, and the crowd broke into applause. She smiled in Jairo's direction and beckoned for him to come forward as many people chanted his name.

"Oh my Lord! What is going on?" Sharon's eyes widened while Mara's gaze remained on Jairo's face.

He smiled somewhat reluctantly before he crossed the room and joined the woman on stage. She welcomed him with a short peck on the lips, then stepped back from the microphone.

Mara and Sharon looked at each other.

Jairo began to speak in Portuguese; then he lapsed into English. "And now I wish to speak to you in English because we have several guests from the United States, and although I don't see them now," he looked as if he were searching for someone, and Sharon tried to push Mara into view, but Mara resisted, "out of respect for them, I feel I must speak in a way that everyone can understand." He looked down. "This is still rather embarrassing for me, even though it's done every once in a while. I'm called up here to speak a little bit about this gathering and how it began." Jairo paused. "But the truth is, it's a very simple thing, and as I've said for many years, the samba is in our blood. It is our life's blood. And for me it was the way that I was able to gain some self-respect in this community. It was a ladder that I climbed outwardly and inwardly. I am very, very happy that the samba school that I started, the Adelina Samba School, has grown in the ways that it has, and that so many people are enjoying it. And," he paused, "that we can put on an event like this. The Adelina Samba School says welcome to whatever other samba schools may be here. Padre Miguel. Tradiciao." He pointed. "Grande Rio. We say welcome and enjoy yourselves, and we shall see you at Carnivale."

The crowd burst into more applause. Jairo turned away from the microphone and the musicians began to play again. As he exited the bandstand the woman slipped her arm through his and they descended the stairs together.

They stepped onto the dance floor, and it was obvious the woman was asking him to dance. Mara saw Jairo decline her offer, but she pulled at him, and began to dance alone.

"*Sim* Jairo," a man encouraged.

"*Sim,*" another voice said.

Mara saw Jairo look at the crowd and smiled as several more people called his name. Then he turned to the woman and began to dance the samba. Although Mara hated to admit it, they were magical together. The moves they executed made Mara aware of how much she did not know about the dance. It was clear from the way Jairo moved that the samba was something he had known for a lifetime, if not more, while the woman knew it so well, she used it openly as an instrument of seduction and enticement. Even though Jairo and the woman were one of many couples on the floor, they stood out from the crowd.

"Well, aren't you glad we didn't compete here in Rio?" a voice said from behind them.

Mara turned to see the overtalkative Vivian with two other contest winners.

"I doubt if any of *us* would have placed," Mara replied.

Vivian gave Mara a dirty look; then her mouth formed a smile that was too silky. "Oh. There's Mr. Camara," she said as if she hadn't seen him. "Do you see him?"

Mara did not reply.

"That man is one dancing machine," Vivian continued. "And the woman he's got with him is giving him more than a run for his money. At least it's obvious she wants to." She chuckled under her breath and glanced at Mara. "I guess, like the rest of us, she needs to stand in line."

The music stopped and there was more applause. Vivian added a loud "Woo-woo!" And many people turned toward the sound, including Jairo and his partner. He said something to his dance partner, then walked toward them.

Chapter 23

"Hello, everyone." Jairo looked at Mara. "I was wondering if you were here."

"We've been here a little while," Vivian said, "and we saw you dance. You are such a dancer."

"Thank you," Jairo replied. "What about you, Mara? How long have you been here?"

"Just a little while." She struggled to keep a nonchalant expression on her face.

"This is the largest crowd yet." He looked around. "Each year more and more people come."

"You seem to have the Midas touch," Sharon said. "It seems no matter what you get involved with turns to gold."

Jairo flashed a brilliant smile. "I don't know about all that."

"But you do have quite a few business interests, don't you?" Vivian asked as the musicians struck up another tune.

"Yes, I do," Jairo answered politely. "But," he pointed behind him, "this is one of my favorite tunes," he said as the slow, sensuous number commenced, "and I'd love to dance to it."

Vivian's eyes grew large with anticipation.

"Mara, would you care to dance with me?"

"Sure." She could hear Vivian's "humpf" as they walked away.

Slowly, Jairo pulled Mara into his arms. "I've been thinking about you all day long," he said near her ear as he moved his body against hers in a slow, erotic fashion.

Mara leaned away from him and looked in his face. "I just bet you have." Then she went forward again.

"You say that as if you don't believe me."

"Let's say from what I've seen since I've been here, I wouldn't stake my life on it."

"And just what is it that you think you have seen?" He put enough distance between them to look down at her through hooded eyes.

"Just you in your element. Always the center of attention. Admired. Desired."

"But that is just the point. When something is an always, as you put it, it loses its luster."

"That's what you say now that it's still happening to you. I bet if all of a sudden all of the attention stopped, you'd be craving it."

Jairo spun Mara out and pulled her back to him. "Who knows?" he said. "But that's not what I want to talk about now. I want to know if you have been thinking about me. About us last night."

"Of course I have." Mara beamed distrust when she looked into his eyes. "I would be a liar if I said I haven't."

His dark eyes watched her. "But you do not think it is the same for me?"

"I don't know." Mara looked down. "I simply don't know."

He tightened his arms about her. "It is. Believe me. It is. I could not get you out of my mind. In business meetings, while going over papers, you were there. Always there, Mara. And so I am looking forward to our getting together tonight."

The music ended and they stopped dancing.

"We'll just have to see, won't we?" Mara turned to walk back to where Sharon stood, but the ends of her mouth curled in a smile.

Jairo took hold of one of her hands. Mara faced him again. "I've got to pay attention to some of the people here, but I don't want to neglect you. Let me help you, Sharon, and the others get seated at one of the tables, and I'll come over and talk to you every once in awhile. Will that do?"

"Possibly." She was feeling her power.

"So now you are going to make me work for you," Jairo said.

"As much as anybody can make the famous Jairo Camara work, I'm sure going to try."

He squeezed her hand and they rejoined Sharon and the others.

"Ladies," Jairo announced. "There is a table right down front. Come with me. I want you to sit and enjoy yourselves." He pulled Mara along. He stopped in front of a table with a "reserved" sign. Jairo promptly removed it.

"It said reserved." Mara's eyebrows rose.

"It is reserved," Jairo replied. "Reserved for you."

Mara couldn't help but smile. "And what do we do when someone comes over here and says this is their table?"

He made his voice low and husky. "Tell them to

talk to me." Then he spoke louder. "Please enjoy yourselves." He bowed and walked away.

The next couple of hours, Jairo kept his word. He would come and check on them, and periodically dance with Mara before he disappeared again.

The evening was in full swing. Several of the women had been asked to dance by Brazilian men, and Mara was feeling quite happy at the amount of attention Jairo was managing to give her. She clapped enthusiastically at a couple who was the current center of attention on the dance floor, but there had been many who exhibited the same level of skill. They all, in Mara's eyes, had been superb.

"You are truly enjoying yourself." She felt a hand on her shoulder.

She looked up into Jairo's face. "I am. It's been a wonderful experience to see the samba danced by so many brilliant dancers. And I finally figured something out."

He knelt beside her. "What is that?"

"That they were calling out the name of the samba school that the best dancers on the floor were associated with. I thought they were saying the people's names." She laughed.

Jairo laughed too. "I'm glad you're happy, and that you have not felt neglected."

"I haven't," she assured him. "I can see that many people want to talk to you, and you have managed to make me feel important in the midst of this."

"You have managed to make the famous Jairo Camara work," he said.

Mara laughed again.

"Jairo."

He stood up.

Mara turned to see the woman in the burnt orange dress.

"Here you are. Over and over you have disappeared." She looked at Mara. "Who are these people, Jairo?"

"They are the group I spoke of from the United States. Some of them are the dancers who won the national contest and a trip to Rio."

"I see." She lifted her chin. "And I am Catarina." She slipped her arm through Jairo's. "Long-time friend, and might as well say family member." She smiled at everyone, but her gaze rested on Mara.

Everyone spoke, but Mara simply smiled slightly.

"I wanted to remind you," she conveniently spoke in English. "I am coming by the house tonight."

"You are?" Jairo's eyes narrowed.

"Yes, I am, and I want you to be there. I didn't know what other business you had planned, but I want you to be there."

"I did have some other plans." Jairo glanced at Mara.

Catarina made a face. "Please. I need you tonight. And don't be too late or I will be worried."

Jairo focused on Catarina's face, then nodded.

"Now come with me. There's a man who wants to speak with you. He says it is important. Can you come now?" She looked at him with steady, long-lashed eyes.

"Sure I can come."

Catarina smiled. "Ladies and gentlemen, I shall take my leave. Enjoy the rest of your evening." Catarina walked away with Jairo in tow.

All eyes at the table were on Mara, and at that moment she couldn't bring herself to face them.

"You want something else to eat?" Sharon came to the rescue.

"That sounds like a good idea." Mara got up and walked over to the food.

Sharon picked up a couple of pastries. She offered one to Mara. Mara took it but she didn't put it in her mouth.

"What is going on with him? Can't he make up his mind?" She looked over at the table.

"What?" Sharon asked defensively. "He has been coming over here to see you. And she had to come and get him."

"Yeah, but when she came to get him, she got him. And she made it plain, in English, for us to see and hear who was in control of that situation."

"I don't know," Sharon replied. "Maybe it is not as simple as it appears."

"You know, it's amazing to me when it comes to Jairo how blind you can be," Mara lashed out. "What else is there?"

Someone touched her arm. She turned. It was Jairo. "You're back."

"Yes. I am back, but I only have a few minutes." He smoothed his hair with his hand. "Perhaps we can meet later than we planned."

"Are you sure you'll be up to it?" Mara snapped.

"Yes, because it is not that kind of thing with Catarina."

"It's not?"

"No."

"Then what is it?"

He looked down, then up again. "It's simply not what you're thinking."

"But you're not going to tell me what it is between you and her?"

"No. I am not. I am simply asking you to trust me."

Mara was stunned. "Maybe this is some kind of cultural gap, but this wouldn't work in America."

Jairo simply looked at her.

Mara closed her eyes. "Now let me get this straight. No matter what I say, you cannot tell me why Catarina is coming to your house, and why you must be there."

Jairo hesitated. "That is what I am saying. But the situation with Cat has nothing to do with you, Mara."

"Cat?" Mara's brow creased. "Cat?" She remembered the phone call Jairo received the first time he sat beside her in the limousine in Orlando.

She looked at Sharon, who looked at her and walked away.

Her heartbeat quickened. "You know, I always considered myself to be rather smart, but I can't claim that anymore. I've been slow when it comes to you. But there is a pattern here." She pressed her fingers against her temple. "Somehow I forgot about the guy that I confronted in the conference room in Orlando. How no matter what I said, he planned to destroy those trees. He didn't give a reason. And he wouldn't budge. It was simply going to be his way or no way at all. And this is what you are telling me now."

He looked at her through heavy lids. "If I take a strong stance, Mara, I always have a good reason."

"Then share it with me," she pleaded. Several people appeared to become interested in what they were talking about.

"I don't choose to do that at this time."

Mara nodded slowly. Her heart was beating so

fast, and she could feel she was about to start shaking. "Okay. Well, I don't choose to see you tonight, Jairo. Or any other evening. I can't do this. Call me scared or whatever." She looked at a woman who was staring down her throat, so Mara stepped closer to him. "When I share myself with a man like I did with you last night, it means quite a lot to me, and it should also mean a lot to him. Because when it comes down to it, how much more could I physically give a human being outside of bearing a child?" She tried to calm herself. "Now, maybe I should have made my old-fashioned notions clearer before last night. But in a case like this, it's best to bring an end to it earlier rather than later." Mara walked away.

"It's time to go," she said to Sharon.

"Again?" Sharon made a face.

"Yes, again. And don't give me any trouble because I'm not in the mood for it."

"Oh, boy. That's what I get for coming to Rio with you." She fell into step behind Mara. "But," Sharon piped up, "I don't mind. A free trip to Rio is a free trip to Rio."

They walked through the ballroom door, through the entrance, and outside.

"At least we did get to have a little bit of fun." She looked at Mara, whose face was set. "A little dancing. A little food. Now back to the old hotel." She paused. "May I assume by your pinched expression you won't be seeing Jairo tonight?"

"You've got that right."

"Wow, I'm some kind of genius," Sharon quipped.

Mara didn't look at her as she stopped a cab, climbed inside, and told the driver where to go.

Sharon sat back and looked at her hands. "Well, Mara, you know I'm not into telling you what to do."

Mara looked at her. "Don't even."

"Well I'm not, usually. So I want you to hear me out." She looked at Mara. "Are you going to hear me out?"

Mara closed her eyes. "Do I have a choice?"

That was good enough for Sharon. "The way I see it, it's obvious that Jairo likes you. And you like him. So whatever life he's had up to this moment is his life, and this woman, Catarina, in the catsuit-like dress has obviously been a part of it. But if he still wants to see you, I don't see what's wrong with enjoying that. Enjoy what he has to offer at this time. I mean, hey." She glanced at Mara. "And it seems to be quite a bit, judging from how happy you were this morning."

"How can it be that simple? It's not," Mara urged. "And when I feel the situation that I seem to be in . . . it feels horrible. It just doesn't feel right."

"Right in what way?" Sharon asked. "He's got a woman here in Brazil, and I'm this woman in America that he wants to see too?"

"That's part of it." Mara folded her hands. "But the truth is, I've never had a man evoke such feelings in me, Sharon. I've dated James for two years, and even wanted to marry him." She shook her head. "And when I think about it now, it's a joke. Because I felt nothing, nothing near what I feel for this man that I've only seen a few times, and have spent only a few hours with."

"Oh-h," Sharon replied.

"Yeah, oh," Mara said. "So I feel if I see Jairo

again, I'm just going to be in deeper trouble emotionally than I already am." She sighed. "I've taken a bite of the forbidden fruit once, and Lord knows what I would feel like if I go back."

Sharon's brow creased. "I think you're in love with him."

Mara opened her mouth to protest, then closed it slowly. "I think I am." She looked at Sharon. "Oh my God, how did I come up with this? To fall in love with Jairo Camara. It makes no sense. It's such an outlandish idea that things will work . . . and I always make sensible decisions."

Sharon touched her arm. "Love isn't always sensible."

"Lord knows in this case it's not. The chance of my having a happy ending is one out of a million. So I'm just going to cut it loose now." Mara hit her knee with her fist.

"I hear you, girl," Sharon replied. "I hear you."

Chapter 24

"Ate logo," Good bye, Jairo said, as he opened the driver's door of his silver Mercedes.

"Ate logo," Eduardo replied. "I'll call you tomorrow morning to set up something with that man we spoke about."

"Sure," Jairo replied. "But I won't get to him tomorrow."

Eduardo closed the car door. "Whatever you say. But tonight was quite a success, no?"

Jairo looked down, then up again. "Overall, I would say yes."

"Ate logo," Eduardo repeated.

"Ate logo." Jairo turned on the car.

"Jairo," Catarina called from behind Eduardo. "Were you going to leave me?"

He looked at her. "I didn't know you intended to ride with me, Catarina."

"Of course I did. I told you I would be coming to your house tonight."

"Yes, but you come over often, and you come on

your own, so I had no idea that I was to take you tonight."

"Is there some problem with that? Do you not want to take me?"

"Catarina," Jairo forced himself to stay in control, "it does not matter. If you are coming, get in the car."

He waited as she walked around the car and climbed into the passenger's seat.

"I must say you are not going to be good company tonight." Catarina closed the door behind her.

"I'm not trying to be."

"And does that little American have something to do with it?"

Jairo looked at her again. "What if she does? I don't see that that's any of your concern."

A beautiful eyebrow lifted. "Well, this conversation has not started out very well." She placed her hand on his thigh. "I don't want to argue with you, Jairo. That is not my way."

Jairo placed Catarina's hand back in her lap and pulled out onto the road. "No, that has not been your approach so far."

"That's because I'm not a mean woman. I prefer to make love and not war." She gazed at him longingly. "If you would only give me a chance to show you how well I know how, I don't think we'd have any more problems like this."

"Catarina, I do not make love, or have sex, or whatever you want to call it, with my sister."

"My goodness. You make it sound so evil. I am your sister, your stepsister, and there is no blood between us. Any babies that came from us would be as normal as God could make them." She pouted.

Jairo continued to look straight ahead. "But we won't be coming up with any babies."

She clicked her tongue. "You're just upset with me now, and I'm not going to talk to you because you are going to hurt my feelings. And I don't want to have such a memory in my mind of my Jairo speaking badly to me. So far you have been very careful of not doing that."

"So far you have not been so . . . what should I call it, outwardly possessive at inappropriate times as you were tonight."

Her eyes blazed. "Who said it was inappropriate? I don't think it was inappropriate. I simply told you I was coming to the house tonight."

"And you picked the perfect opportunity. Just as I was visiting with Mara—"

"Is that her name, Mar-ra? What does it mean? Probably nothing." She crossed her arms. "Not like our names—"

"Catarina." Jairo shook his head.

"Visiting with her. You visited with her on and off all through the evening."

Jairo glanced at Catarina, then back at the road. "And that is my prerogative. To do what I please, to visit with whom I please."

"Of course it is, but what is it that she has that I don't have? From what I could see, I have much more in the right places."

"What she has, Catarina," Jairo replied, "you cannot just see with the eyes. But in addition to that," he paused, "I think she is beautiful."

She dusted off her dress. "You and your thinking. I never knew you had so many thoughts. You've never shown them to me, and you most definitely have not shown them to poor Benedito. Your father. Our father."

Jairo's eyes narrowed. "I have shown him as much feeling as I can muster at this time in my life, and that is the only reason I allow him to live with me."

"You allow him to?" Catarina vented her anger. "It is your duty to take care of your father. It's not allowing."

"I allow him to live with me," Jairo repeated. "And that is more than he did for my mother and me, when I was a baby and a boy growing up. So do not preach to me about duties to a father who was never there."

"See," she pointed. "Now this I've seen before. These kind of feelings I've seen before. But this other that you are showing for this Mara are unfamiliar to me."

Jairo did not reply.

But that didn't stop Catarina. "And on top of that, you act as if my coming to the house is some kind of imposition. I come all the time."

"Yes, you come all the time. And why? Why do you come? To see our father?" Jairo gave her a look that said none of the reasons she came to the house were good reasons.

"Yes, I come to see Benedito." She lifted her chin. "Just as I am coming to see him tonight."

"Why?" he pressed.

"Because he asked me to. Because he needs me. Because I show him the care that you refuse to give him."

Jairo glanced at the clock. "I bet by now he wouldn't know if you were giving him care, or setting him on fire."

"Believe me, he knows." She tightened her arms. "He knows all of it."

"How can you be so sure, Catarina? How can you?"

"Because he talks to me as he talks to no other. He says I listen to him and I respect him."

"And when does he do this talking?"

Catarina looked down. "Sometimes we talk in the morning over coffee when you are not there. But there are other times, too."

"But how do you know what he tells you is the truth, because he may not remember a word of it later?" Jairo glanced her way.

She shook her head. "See, you give him no credit, Jairo. Because our father drinks a little it does not make him some kind of a monster."

"My father," he separated each word, "drinks a hell of a lot. He drinks all the time. He's an alcoholic that has almost drunk himself to death. And that is why he cannot take care of himself. Let alone a family. And that is why *your* mother kicked him out."

"She put him out because he was unfaithful to her." Catarina looked out the window.

"Infidelity. Let's add that to his list of virtues," Jairo replied.

"I cannot focus on all of the things he has done wrong because I remember how he was with me when I was a little girl," Catarina said. "He was kind to me, and he gave me a beautiful home. I wanted for nothing."

Jairo's tone went solemn. "I'm glad you have such good memories, Cat. Because when I was a little boy, I constantly wondered if I even had a father, while my mother and I lived hand to mouth.

Then I found out my father was some grand aristocrat here in Rio, living a life that I could not have dreamed of at the time."

"But he was young then, and he had made a mistake that affected his whole life."

"That's right." Jairo looked at her. "I was his mistake. Had he met my mother and she had not gotten pregnant, then this *mistake* of his would have just gone on as a quiet lay with a poor woman. But I came along, and when everyone found out about it, when his image was tarnished by the truth, then he began to drink. So he was young, and the mistake he made by getting my mother pregnant, and my being born turned him into the drunk that he is. So it's all my fault, is that what you're saying?"

"Of course not." She touched his arm. "I'm simply saying you must forgive him, Jairo. He's an old man now."

Jairo sighed. "I have forgiven as much as I can. And that is why I am allowing," he paused, "my father to live in my house. That is as much as I can forgive." He pulled up in into his driveway.

"With this line drawn in the sand between you," she opened the car door, "how can there be forgiveness? It is not good for you, and it is not good for him." She closed the door behind her.

"Catarina." Jairo sighed again. "Don't make it your job to decide what is good and bad for me. You should focus on your own life." He joined her on the other side of the car. "All of these recent antics of yours, trying to lure me in to your web, are not good for either one of us."

She tossed her head. "I think that there is nothing wrong with my finding my brother, I mean

stepbrother, attractive, and that our coming together would be good for this family."

"I disagree." Jairo opened the door and Catarina
stepped inside.

"Oh no," Catarina moaned.

Jairo looked. Benedito lay sprawled on the floor,
a bottle of spilled whiskey not far from his hand.

Catarina rushed to his side.

"I guess you won't be doing any talking tonight."
Jairo knelt down, picked his father up and started
toward his father's room. Catarina walked beside
him as Benedito's head lolled back and forth.
"They've told him his liver is eaten up with alcohol. So why does he continue to drink like this?"
Jairo asked as they entered his father's bedroom.

"Perhaps it's because he knows his one and only
blood son has never forgiven him."

Jairo laid Benedito on the bed. He looked at
Catarina. "Just as Benedito has waited until it was
too late for the doctors to fix his liver, he has waited
until it was too late to repair the heart of the boy
that he hurt so badly long ago."

Chapter 25

"I thought about just stopping by since you refused to answer my phone calls." Jairo's voice came
over the message service. "But I don't know if you
really want me to. And I don't want to invade your
space. I don't want to disrespect you. So . . . call
me, Mara. That's if you want to. *Ate logo.*"

Afterward Mara listened to the voice trying to
decide whether to save the message or erase it. She
chose to erase it.

Mara stood up from the bed and noticed that
Sharon was standing not far away. "Hey."

"Hey," Sharon replied. "So he called again, did
he?"

"Yeah." Mara looked at the telephone. "He
called again."

"Wow. I have to give it to you. You're one strong
woman. You know that?"

Mara crossed her arms. "I'm a woman trying to
save herself some heartache. And when I think
about it, if Jairo had come here, that night, after

the dance, I would not have had the strength to keep him out. But with the few days that have passed by, and with him calling and not just coming near me," she made a circle around her, "I've gained some strength, and I'm not going to call him back. I'm not." She looked at Sharon with conviction. "I'm going to enjoy the rest of my stay here in Rio, and I'm going to go back to the States and be thankful, like you said, for the good times. And I'll remember this for the rest of my life. That this Brazilian millionaire was attracted to me." She laughed a little. "So when I look at my little rugrats by some ordinary guy, and I'm into the routine of doing average things that married women in America do, I can always look back on this and say, 'I had my Cinderella moment.' But I'll still know that I made the right choice."

"Wow. You are the planner," Sharon replied.

Mara smiled. "Yep, I always have been."

"Well, I've got some plans for today." Sharon waved a small sheet of paper.

"You do?"

"Yeah. We've been invited to Roberto's family's house today. I spoke to him on the phone last night, and he's set it up with them. He says the majority of his family speaks good English, so communication shouldn't be a problem."

"Really?" Mara was grateful for something different to do.

"Yeah. And he says when you look at his folks you think you are looking at the United Nations, there are so many skin colors. And Roberto says they'll treat us well. He's given me the directions." She waved the paper again. "I wrote them down, but he told me to check with the hotel concierge, so they can map it out for us. Roberto says it shouldn't be any problem taking a cab, but he warned me not to expect any lush surroundings because they actually live in the countryside. Still, he says he grew up in a house full of love," she smiled, "full of tradition, and that we should have a good time."

"Sounds great." But Mara's thoughts turned to Jairo.

"What's that face?" Sharon asked.

"I was just wondering if you and Roberto have discussed what's been going on with Jairo and me."

"Just a bit. It's not that I haven't tried to pick him for information," Sharon confessed. "But Roberto seems to be reluctant to go into depth about Jairo. I know they practically grew up together, so I don't know if it's because Jairo is the big, big boss or what, but when it comes to him Roberto is very protective. He says things like 'He's a good man,' and 'You can't judge him by what you see now.' And he feels Jairo deserves happiness. That kind of stuff." She shrugged. "He won't get down and dirty like I want him to."

"He's protecting his friend," Mara replied.

"Yeah, I guess so." Sharon smiled again. "But either way, we've got plans." She waved the paper again. "We have been shopping and to the beach so many times I can't even count, and I am looking forward to this."

A couple of hours later they were in a cab on their way to the countryside.

"Sir. Sir," Sharon slapped the back of the seat near the taxi driver. "Could you slow down, please? I'm going to scream in a minute if we go around another road like this, where we could just drop off the edge and be killed at any minute, and you're taking it like you're on a racetrack."

The driver grinned in the mirror as he'd done during milder admonitions from Sharon. "I'm sorry. I'm sorry. But I am so accustomed to driving like this. Believe me, you are safe. No problem."

"I hear you, but my heart does not believe you. It's beating so fast that it's about to pop out of my chest. I will believe you when you slow down," Sharon railed.

"Okay." He smiled and gazed at her through the mirror.

"Oh my God! Watch it! Watch it!" Mara yelled.

The driver looked at the road and swerved out of the way of another vehicle, driving just as fast.

"See, you are in good hands," he assured them. "This is how we drive here."

Mara's hand was still over her heart, and Sharon was wiping perspiration from her forehead. "I see, and it scares me to death. Where are the yellow lines?"

He looked puzzled. "What are these yellow lines?"

"The yellow lines that are supposed to be in the middle of the road that says, this is our side, and that is their side."

"We don't need them," he replied innocently.

"I don't want to hear any more," Mara said. "In this case, the less I know the better off I am."

Sharon sat back. "Me too. I'm going to get to Roberto's parents home and never want to leave. If it's going to be like this coming back. And it will be dark then; I don't know what I'm going to do."

But the driver proved true to his word this time, and slowed down. That didn't make the few cars driving behind them very happy, and they showed their displeasure by making daring passes. With all the excitement, the fun of sightseeing had waned, and the driver's explanations of the farms that they passed fell on deaf ears.

"This is the turnoff that is marked on your map. This is the place." He pulled off onto the dirt road.

Sharon made the sign of the cross in front of her body, although she was no Catholic. "I'm so glad we're here."

"You're not the only one." Mara looked out at the farmhouse.

The taxi pulled up beside a vintage Caprice that had been restored and kept in impeccable condition, and an old truck that had not.

Mara opened her purse so she could help pay for the bill.

"No," Sharon stopped her. "This is my treat. Roberto said he is going to reimburse whatever it cost to get here."

"Roberto's turning out to be quite the honey," Mara said.

She waited for Sharon to pay; then they got out of the car. Sharon started toward the house, but Mara held on to the vehicle through the open window. "Wait a minute. I want to make sure we are in the right place before you leave us out here."

"Now that's a good idea," Sharon replied as the driver nodded.

No sooner than that was said, the screen door of the house opened. A heavyset woman in her mid-fifties stepped outside. "You Sharon?" She looked at Sharon and then at Mara.

"Yes, I'm Sharon."

The woman broke into a warm smile. "Welcome. Welcome," she said. "We have been waiting for you."

Chapter 26

Sharon smiled at the woman. "Glad to hear that. So this is the place." She looked at Mara, who turned toward the taxi.

Mara looked at her watch. "Come back in a couple of hours."

He nodded, and pulled off in a patch of dust.

"And you?"

"I'm Mara, Sharon's friend."

The woman nodded enthusiastically. "Yes, we have been waiting for you, Sharon. I am Roberto's mother, Sabina. Roberto told me he invite you to our dinner, I pleased but surprised."

"Really?" Sharon replied.

"Yes. Roberto no do this before."

"I don't know what to say." Sharon glanced at Mara before she looked at Sabina again. "I guess I should feel good about that."

"You should." Sabina's eyes were serious. "Because Roberto's family very important to him. And he not send anyone here he no feel good about."

"Wow." Sharon looked humbled.

"Come inside," Sabina motioned. "There are few family people here. My husband, children, and family friend has come too. But he like family. We do this every year and he come. But we simple people, no fancy. I hope you no disappointed."

Sharon stood in the door. "Well, I've never been on a farm before, and to visit my first one here in Brazil, I'm just excited, period." Sharon's face turned sincere. "And I feel honored to be invited to spend time with Roberto's family."

"Ah-h, you are a good girl." Sabina patted Sharon's cheek. "I'm going to like you. Like you a lot. So come. Come inside. Everyone in back." She led them inside. "My house, small house, but full of love." She looked at Mara.

"I'm sure," Mara replied. "I'm sure it is."

"We going to eat on porch in back of kitchen. Outside. It nice and cool out there," Sabina explained as she walked. "We eat there all the time we come together."

They walked through a living area and a kitchen and emerged outside.

"Roberto's friends have come," Sabina announced.

There were several greetings and smiles from the small group sitting at a picniclike table.

"Now let me go around and introduce," Sabina said. "But first this, Sharon."

"The woman Roberto has been talking about," a man who looked a lot like Roberto said.

"Yes," Sabina pointed. "This is the one. And this is her friend Mara." Mara waved. "Here we have my husband, Roberto's father, Sergio. And over here the twins, Livia and Livius. Did Roberto tell you he had a twin brother and sister?"

"Yes, he told me." Sharon smiled.

Sabina continued. "Yes, Livius and Livia. Livius is married to Juliana." She introduced an attractive young woman sitting next to Livius. "And this, Gualter, my sister's son."

Greetings were exchanged.

"And my special son is here but he—oh, perfect. Here he comes. Jairo, I want you to meet Sharon and Mara."

"I know them," Jairo looked at Mara.

Sabina covered her mouth with her hand. "No. But I guess it is possible because Roberto mentioned that he met you, Sharon, through the dance school."

"Yes, that is how we met." Sharon looked from Mara to Jairo.

"So this is good. Jairo is a member of our family too." Sabina threw up her arms. "Now sit, sit, sit. The food is ready and on the table. We are simply waiting for you. Sit, sit, sit."

Roberto's father patted the space beside him. "You sit here, Sharon. I want to get to know this American woman that my son has sent to my house." He sounded serious but his face betrayed him.

Mara sat in an empty space at the other end. Jairo sat beside her.

"This is quite unusual." Jairo spoke so only Mara could hear. "It seems as if fate has something in store for us no matter how much you want to change it."

"I have nothing against fate." Mara shook her

head. It was uncanny that Jairo was there. "But sometimes fate can be quite cruel." She looked at the people sitting around the table. "I'm simply looking out for myself."

"We've got good but simple food today." Sabina interrupted their private exchange. "And it is quite filling. I hope you like it. It's called *feijoada*. We say it is our Brazilian national dish. We eat it all the time, so I thought it would be good for you to have it here at my home." Sabina sat down. "It's got black beans, beef, and pig ears and tails. I don't know if you have ever had them before." Her eyes sparkled. "It also has pork sausage and chops, salt pork, and a little bacon. As you can see we like our meat, our pork." She rubbed her chin. "And let me see what else, oranges, and limes and chili peppers, bay leaves, onion, garlic, and rice. I think you'll like it very much. You should not be hungry after this. But you must save room for the little sweet that I prepared. It's *doce*, what you would call a fruit jelly. It's made from guava, and it's really good with cheese. So please. Please. You are our guests, be first."

Mara looked at the large steamy dish of the stew-like concoction, then looked at Sharon who was avidly engaged in a conversation with Roberto's father, Sergio.

"Here," Jairo said, "let me help you." He picked up her bowl, stood up, and filled it. He set it in front of her.

"What type of drink would you like?" Jairo indicated a collection of bottles. "There is homemade *cachaca*, which is the best kind, fruit juice and *refrigerantes*, sodas."

"Oh, I forgot something inside," Sabina said.

"We've also got *guarana*. It is made from berries that come from a shrub in the rainforest. It gives you energy."

Mara looked at the array of drinks. "Well, I think I'll have some *guarana,*" Mara replied. "I think I'm going to need all the energy I can get."

Mara and Jairo looked at each other.

"Sergio," Sabina called sharply. "Let Sharon get some food first before you talk her to death and the food gets cold. You will ruin the *feijoada*. Here, now that Mara has her food, let me serve you, Sharon."

"No," Sergio said. "I'll do it. I forgot my manners."

"Everybody is so nice," Sharon said as he took her bowl and ladled a full serving of *feijoada*.

"Jairo has already helped your friend here. Your name again?" Sergio asked.

"Mara," Mara said.

"Your friend, Mara. And mother is pushing me to feed you. But you know why?" He leaned toward Sharon.

"No." Sharon shook her head.

"Because she is hungry. I know her. She is ready to eat the whole thing herself."

Sabina slapped his arm. "Don't you embarrass me so quickly."

Everyone laughed, and Mara watched as the *feijoada* was served.

"By the way, Jairo," Gaulter said. "How is Catarina?"

Mara glanced at Jairo, but he focused on Gaulter. "She is fine."

A crooked smile appeared. "That I know."

Jairo smiled a little as Gaulter laughed.

"I saw her the other day, in Rio. I spoke to her and she tolerated me but that was about all."

"Well, you know Catarina," Jairo replied.

"But I wish I could get to know her better. She's so fixed in your direction."

"Gaulter, you've known Cat as long as I have. She's like a pit bull. Once she attaches to something, gets her mind set, it's hard to shake her loose. But she is also as fickle as they come. Who knows what the future will hold," Jairo continued. "Even a pit bull can't hold on forever."

"So true," Gaulter remarked. "So true."

Livius, who sat across from Jairo, accepted a bowl of stew from his wife, Juliana. "So, you know each other already," he said after several mouthfuls.

"Yes, we do," Jairo said.

Mara simply nodded.

"Is this not a small world? So how do you know each other?" Livius asked. "I know that Roberto met Sharon at the dance school. Is this also the situation?"

"That's exactly how we met," Mara replied. "Through Roberto's dance school."

"Roberto's dance school." He stuck his index finger in the air. "But you know that Jairo, he is the man who has all these dance schools in America."

"Yes, I know," Mara managed to say with her mouth full.

Livius continued. "He is the man, I tell you. We are so proud to be like family for him. Here in Rio," he made a gesture with his mouth and rolled his eyes, "Jairo is like gold. Everyone wants a piece of him. But look at him. Look at him. This is the Jairo we know. He comes here, he has on his jeans and plain T-shirt. He does not come chauffeured in the limousine."

Mara looked at Jairo. There was a different air about him. Unlike the dinner and the dance, in this atmosphere Jairo looked surprisingly relaxed. He looked at Mara and continued to eat.

"That's right, there was no limousine out front," Mara said.

"That was his Caprice. You saw Caprice?" Livius asked. "We worked on it here at the house. It's in beautiful shape."

"It's a great-looking car," Mara replied.

"That's because Jairo and I," he motioned between them, "worked on it here at the house. Jairo, we did good, huh?"

Jairo smiled. "Yes, Livius. We did good."

"It's kind of hard to picture Jairo working under the hood of a car, huh?" He looked at Mara.

Mara stopped eating. "To be honest with you, I am surprised."

"Don't be," Sabina said. "Jairo, he is just a regular person. And we know that, because we have known him for a long, long time. But all these other people, after they get to know Jairo, or they hear of Jairo and find out about all the money that he has. And I tell you," She waved her empty spoon in the air, "he's very rich, very rich."

"Please, Mama Sabina." Jairo looked at her.

She put up her hand. "No, no, no, it's true. He's a regular person, but they won't let him be a regular person. They insist that he drive in a limousine. He says, 'I want to drive my car.' I've seen it. I've seen it happen. 'I want to drive my own car. I can drive my own car.' 'No, no, no, Mr. Camara. You cannot drive your own car. It is not good for business. You must have an image.' You must do this. You must do that. So what does Jairo do?" She raised her shoulders. "He submits."

"Really?" Mara replied.

"Yes." She gave Jairo a pitiful look.

"And how long have you known each other?" Mara asked.

"It's been almost twenty-five years now, I would think. Huh, Sergio?"

"Yes, I would say that long."

"You want to hear how I met Jairo?" Sabina asked.

"I would love to hear it," Mara replied.

Chapter 27

"I was in the city, in Rio, and a group of kids, what I think you call street kids—"

"Yes, I understand," Mara said.

"Yes," Sabina nodded. "I was doing a little shopping and these kids, they come and they take my purse. Roberto was with me. He was a young boy too. Maybe nine at the time. And I'm crying, I'm crying because it is all my money. I have no more money. I have no more money and they have taken my purse." She shook her head. "So Roberto, he, no matter my telling him no, he go after the boys to get back my purse. And my goodness, they had scattered by then, but he caught the one who had my purse." Her eyes grew large. "And those boys they come back and they attack my Roberto. And then I see this young boy come out, and he comes and pushes them off of my Roberto, and he demands that they stop. And by then, of course, I am over there with more people, and they make that boy give me back my purse." She exhaled. "I am very happy then, but I hear the boys shout, 'Jairo, we think you think you better than us. You no better than us. You live on the street too, but you think you better than us because you dance to get some money. You think you better because you no take things from people, but you are the same as us. You remember that.' And they spit at him." She looked at Mara. "You know?"

"No, I didn't know," Mara said as she looked at Jairo. Her chest felt tight.

"Yes. This is true," Sergio chimed in. "Jairo, this mighty man here, he was a street kid. He was one of them, but he no want to do crime. He no want to do crime. He determined he would find another way to make money. And he did." He shook his finger. "He was dancing. He would make enough money to eat. This is the kind of boy he was without parent. This is the kind of boy he was," Sergio repeated.

"So," Sabina took the ball again, "at that time I say to him, I say, you live here? You no have home? You live on the street? And Jairo would not answer me. He would not. And I ask again, you live on street? He would not answer me. But there was a man who sold food in the area, and he say this one live on the street too. But he no like the others. 'If I had the room, but I live here in the city, it's so crowded. If I had the room, I would take this one in because I have watched him, and he is a good boy. A good boy. Life has just not smiled on him.' "

Mara glanced at Jairo, but he was looking at Sabina.

"Then I saw Jairo get this kind of shy look, so shy, you know. He was like backing up and walking away like he was going to leave us. And I say no,

no, you wait. You wait. You must come with us."
She knotted her fists over her heart. "My heart
went out to him so strong. I could just feel my
heart when looking at this boy, who look not much
older than my Roberto. And I say, I've got kids, several kids, but we always have room for one more. I
live on farm. I no live here in the city. You come
home with me. You come with us. But at first Jairo
refuse." Sabina looked upset. "And I said, no, I will
not leave this place until you come with me. I cannot leave you here like this. Come." She looked at
Mara. "His eyes done something to me inside. I
could not leave him there. And this is how Jairo
came to stay with us for a while."

"And so he comes back here," Livius picked up
the story, "and he does live with us. But he and I we
always fighting. Always fighting. You know why?"

"Why?" Sharon asked.

"Because I am jealous of this fellow."

Jairo chuckled.

"He laughs now, but he knows I was. I was jealous because he could dance so well, and all the
girls loved him because he could dance. So whenever there was a contest or something of that kind,
we would want to go because there would be girls
there, and Jairo would show off. My mother said
he was shy on that street, later he wasn't shy."

Mara giggled at Livius's expression.

"He would dance. If there was a contest," Livius
pointed at Jairo, "everybody would ask if Jairo was
coming. And he would compete and he would
win. Sometimes Roberto would win too. But me,"
he shook his head, "never. Still, Jairo won so
much, his name would be in the papers, because
here in Brazil dancing is so much a part of our cul-

ture. It is a beautiful part of us. You can ride the wings of the samba and your name can become famous in Rio."

Mara nodded as she listened.

"So, I got lucky sometimes with the girls because Jairo was there, but fate was good to him. Dancing is one thing, but you could never do what Jairo has done with all these companies and such, unless you were smart. And Jairo was smart. I don't want you to think that he was this dancing, good-looking man that you see now." Livius took another spoonful of stew.

"Thank God for *feijoada*," Jairo said.

"This is the part he does not like to talk about." Livius continued with his mouth full. "So out of respect for him I will not give the details. But one day, fate smiled on him, and he ended up going to school, a good private school for boys." Livius's eyebrows rose. "And from there Jairo took hold of opportunity and started his first dance school here in Rio. It was not for street kids or poor people like us. We already know how to samba. Jairo understood that the high class, the rich people, they want to dance like us. To move their hips like us." He laughed. "To dance to the music that is rich with flavor and movement. Not that upper-class stiff stuff." Livius wrinkled his nose. "They want to samba. So Jairo made samba schools available to them, you know. And he made jobs available to some of the poorer people that he knew were good dancers, and would know how to mingle with the other half." Livius dipped another spoonful of *feijoada*. "But I can tell by his face that he has gotten tired of all this talk, and I don't want him to stop coming by here and escaping his rich life." He laughed again.

"That will never happen," Jairo said.

All of Roberto's family laughed.

"So what do you two do in America?" Gaulter looked at Sharon.

"I work for the city of Orlando, in the probate court clerk's office. Basically, I do secretarial work, but it is good. The city has been good to me. I have great benefits."

"Yes, America can have good benefits. We know," Gaulter replied. "You are very fortunate to have such a job."

"I think I am," Sharon said. "And it was because of all my vacation time that I was able to come here, courtesy of Mara."

"So Mara was the reason that you are here?" Gaulter asked.

"She is," Sharon replied.

"And Mara, you just came for vacation?" Gaulter turned up a brown bottle.

"Actually, the trip was a gift." She hesitated, "It came out of my being a part of a dance contest." She managed to tell the truth. "A samba dance contest."

"So you are a dancer too," Sabina said. "You and Jairo seem to get along pretty well." She looked at both of them. "We must see you and him dance before you leave."

"I don't think so," Mara replied.

Jairo smiled.

"What kind of work do you do?" Gaulter continued.

"I do design consultant work."

Sabina's brow creased.

"In other words, I help people make decisions about what materials to use on their buildings, and how to make the outside of the structure, and the surrounding area, more attractive," Mara said. "That kind of thing."

"Sounds impressive," Sabina said.

"Not really." Mara looked down.

"You must be very smart to do such a job," Livius said. "I thought most of that is done by men."

"I work with a few men. But I think I'm able to hold my own."

"Talk about Jairo, now she is being shy," Sharon said. "Mara can hold her own with anyone. In her field you won't find anyone better."

Mara smiled. "You can tell we've been friends for a long time. I blackmail her into saying things like that."

Sabina looked surprised until everyone laughed; then she laughed too.

Mara continued eating, but her mind was going over the things that had been said about Jairo. How he had grown up. She wondered about his parents, better still his lack. He was on her mind so deeply, Mara would stop in the middle of eating and just gaze at her food, not seeing it at all.

"Is the food okay?" Sergio asked at one of those lapses.

Mara looked at him. "Yes. Yes, it's good. Thank you. I've been wondering," she attempted to cover her tracks, "what kind of farm this is."

"It's been a soybean farm for many years," Sergio replied. "We did okay. Enough to feed our family, but things got pretty hard and we were having a little trouble. But thanks to Jairo we were able to buy several head of cattle, because we had good grazing land here. That was about three, four years ago?" He looked at Jairo.

Jairo nodded.

"Yes, three four years ago," Sergio continued. "And we are doing some cattle farming now. It is much better for us. More money is coming in, and we are feeling much better for it."

"My goodness," Sharon said. "Jairo you sound like a hero all the way around."

"It's because they love me that they make me sound that way." He looked around the table and smiled.

"We do love you, Jairo. We do. We do." Sabina blew him several kisses. "You're just like a son."

Chapter 28

The meal continued with lots of laughter, jokes at everyone's expense, and probing glances between Jairo and Mara. Jairo's eyes appeared serene as he looked deep within her, whereas Mara's gaze was confused.

The group began to break up after the *doce* with cheese was consumed.

"Let me show you something," Mara heard Sergio say as he got up from the table. He touched Sharon on the shoulder. "You say you are interested in guitars?"

"I am. I've even tried to play a little," Sharon replied. "But I'm not very good at it."

"I've got something special for you," he replied. "I want to show you a guitar that has been in our family for a long time. And Roberto plays a guitar pretty well. Did you know that?"

Sharon smiled. "He's bragged about it, but I've never heard him play."

Sergio laid his finger against his nose. "Next

time you see him, you tell him, his father says, 'You play this woman some music.' Tell him just like that. Because it is one of the most powerful persuaders I know." He laughed vigorously.

"All right, Sergio," Sabina warned from the kitchen.

Sergio laid his finger against his lips and Sharon followed him into the house. Mara got up from the table as well and walked over to a large shade tree. She looked out over the land. Physically, she was full and content, but more than food had been placed on Mara's table. It was such a normal dinner, she thought. The food was different and the accents were different, but the conversation and the laughter and family love were familiar. Mara couldn't help but think about how well Jairo fit in. Here, he wasn't the multimillion-dollar businessman. It wasn't an issue. At least for him it didn't appear to be. He was simply a man enjoying the company of people he loved and who obviously loved him. Mara looked at the tree and began to pick the bark.

"Disappointed?" Jairo said softly from behind her.

Mara glanced over her shoulder. "What?"

"Disappointed that I'm not the heartless, take-advantage-of-innocent-people, that you made me out to be?"

"No, I'm not disappointed at all. I never thought you were heartless, Jairo. That wasn't what . . . frightened me. And frightened is the right word. I just didn't want to be a part of the game that you seem to play." She gazed out over the land again. "All the women that you meet across the globe," she said. "I don't want to be one of those links in that chain. It wouldn't do me any good in the long run, and even though there may be some fun to be had, it's just not enough for me. It's not enough."

"Just because I travel, Mara, and, as you say, meet all kinds of people, women, it doesn't mean I take up with all of them."

She leaned against the tree before she looked up at his face. Her somewhat skeptical expression said it all.

"I don't. Now, when I was younger, my God," Jairo closed his eyes and shook his head, "I was a bumblebee trying to pollinate every flower, but you know it gets a little old. Especially, when you realize, even though pleasure was being received, I was also being used."

"Poor Jairo," Mara teased.

"No, seriously. Some of them wanted me as a boyfriend because of what I could buy them, what I could offer, or where I could take them. Some of them, with money, wanted more, for me to be their husband because they felt it would give them some prestige here in Rio." He looked at her matter-of-factly. "Mind you, these were not women from the older established families, these were women who were from families of new money. So my days of being with one woman after another . . . ended not too long ago. But regardless of when it ended, Mara, it did." He traced the small of her back with his hand.

Mara felt heat spread throughout her body.

"So I must admit, I'm very happy that circumstance would make it that I would see you here. Like this."

"And Roberto didn't tell you that I was going to be here?"

"No, he did not tell me. I could easily ask, Roberto did not tell Sharon, and she didn't tell you, that *I* would be here?" he challenged.

She shrugged. "Now seriously, if you had known that I was going to be here, would you still have come?"

Jairo looked out over the land. "I would have thought it over beforehand, because probably contrary to your belief, my feelings can be hurt too. I can only take a certain amount of rejection without lashing out in some way. Or I might even retreat. Would you want that?" he asked softly.

It was Mara's turn to hesitate. "No, I wouldn't want that at all."

They stood and watched the wind blow through the trees before Mara turned her attention to Juliana, who was clearing the table.

"How do you like this part of Brazil?" Jairo asked.

"I like it. Roberto has a beautiful family. And I guess, in a way, my saying that about them, means I am saying it about you too. They see you as a part of them."

"I am," Jairo replied. "They have been the only real family that I've known."

Mara wished Jairo would say more about his family, but he did not.

"So," she couldn't help herself, "from what Sabina said you were actually orphaned at one point."

He nodded as he looked at the land. "Yes, I was an orphan living on the streets."

"My goodness." Mara looked at him. "That must have been very hard."

"It definitely was one of the harder times, but as you can see I survived it."

"But how old were you?" Mara pressed.

"When I met Sabina and Roberto?"

Mara nodded.

"I was eleven years old."

"Eleven," Mara repeated. "So what happened? Did your parents die in an accident or did whoever was taking care you of die suddenly?"

"It was no accident," Jairo replied. "My mother was murdered, and up until that point, my father had never been a part of my life."

"Oh." Jairo's dry tone made Mara feel uncomfortable. "Do you have any brothers and sisters?"

"No, there is only me. At least when it comes to blood brothers and sisters."

"Hey, Jairo," Gaulter called across the yard.

"Yes."

"Can I get a ride back with you to Rio?"

"Sure," Jairo replied. He looked at Mara. "Will you two need a ride as well?"

"We told the cab driver to come back in about thirty minutes. We didn't know how long we'd actually be here."

"I'll give you two a ride back. I'll call the cab company and cancel your reservation."

"That will work." Mara removed his card from her pocket. "Sharon and I were dreading riding back with that guy, he drove much too fast."

"Don't speak too quickly you haven't been in a car with me." He smiled. "That's how we drive here in Rio."

It was obvious to Mara that Jairo was glad the conversation had changed, and although she longed to know more, she wouldn't press it.

The good-byes before they left were simple and sincere with lots of hugs to go around.

"We want to see you back here again, Sharon," Sergio said. "Next time with Roberto, if you can still stomach him and all his craziness by that time."

"I think I'll be able to," Sharon replied.

"Really?" Sabina put her hands on her hips. "I think you really like my son."

"I do," Sharon admitted. "And being here with you reminded me of the times I've been to Puerto Rico. Our culture is different from yours, but not so different."

"We do look forward to you coming back." Sabina hugged Sharon. "And Mara, I did not get to spend a lot of time with you because Jairo occupied the majority of your conversation. Am I not right, Jairo?"

"You are always right." He gave her a kiss on the cheek.

"Could it be," she scratched her arm, "that two of my boys have fallen for girls who live in America?"

"Anything's possible, Mama Sabina. My proof is you fell for this fellow." Jairo shook Sergio's hand before he gave him a bear hug.

"You are right," Sabina said, and she and Sergio laughed.

The final good-byes were said and Jairo and Mara climbed into the front seat of the Caprice, while Sharon and Gaulter entered the back.

Jairo drove while they talked continuously about Rio, Brazil, dancing, food, and the difference between Brazil and the United States. Mara talked, but her thoughts were rehashing what she had heard and seen at Roberto's family home. Finally,

Jairo pulled up in front of a somewhat tall apartment building.

"Here you are, Gaulter. Safe and sound," Jairo said.

Gaulter squeezed Jairo's shoulder over the seat. "Yes, I can always depend on you. I'll be forever in your debt."

"Oh sure," Jairo said playfully.

"It was nice meeting both of you. Mara."

"Good to meet you too, Gaulter."

"Sharon." He took her hand and patted it. "I wish you had time to come with me and meet some more of the family. I've got one brother that you would swear was Roberto. They look like twins."

"You're kidding," Sharon said.

"No kidding. Am I right, Jairo?"

"He's telling the truth. He looks just like Roberto."

"Really." Sharon looked amused.

"And see, if you had time, you could come with me and we could go by my brother's home and visit with us a little more."

"I'd like that," Sharon said. "Mara, we don't have any more plans today, do we?"

Mara turned in the seat. "No, we don't."

"Okay then, I think I'm going to go with Gaulter, and I'll see you later tonight."

"That's fine, Sharon. Go on and have a good time."

Sharon and Gaulter got out of the car on opposite sides. Gaulter motioned for Jairo to roll down his window.

Gaulter leaned in close. "I'm sorry if I messed

up something with you and Mara when I mentioned Catarina. I didn't realize that—"

"Don't worry. It's no problem."

"You know I'm always messing around."

"You're okay, Gaulter." Jairo patted his face.

"All right then. It was good to meet you, Mara." He projected his voice.

"You as well, Gaulter." Then she waved at Sharon before they walked away.

Chapter 29

The car grew silent before Jairo said, "Now it's just the two of us again."

"It is," Mara replied.

"And seeing you don't have any plans and neither do I, would you mind if I came to your suite? We could listen to some music and talk for awhile."

Mara thought about Jairo's offer, and she thought about Gaulter's whispered apology. "You must really like hotels," she said.

Jairo rested his arm across the seat behind her. "No, I simply want to spend more time with you."

Mara sighed. "There are all kinds of ways of doing that, besides sitting in my hotel room."

"What do you suggest?" His expression appeared more guarded. *I don't believe he is forcing me to say this.* She looked Jairo dead in the eyes. "I'd love to see . . ." Then Mara changed her mind. "Look Jairo, although Gaulter thought he was whispering, I heard him, and what he said about Cat. I know I haven't known you that long. And I realize you had a life before you met me, if there is a me at this point." She looked down and up again. "When I think about it, I think about how I've spent my life trying not to be in the middle of stuff like this. And, I just . . . it's not my cup of tea."

"What are you talking about?" Jairo's forehead creased.

"This whole thing with you and Catarina."

"What about me and Cat?"

Mara exhaled in frustration. "Jairo, I told you—"

"Yes, you heard Gaulter. You heard what Gaulter said earlier, and you heard what he said just then. But you don't know what's going on here."

"And when I tried to find out at the dance, you refused to tell me," she retorted. "But it's pretty obvious to me."

"Is it?"

"It is," Mara replied. "You've gone through all this trouble to bring me to Rio, set me up in a master suite, so you can be with me there. Even though you have a home here, you've not invited me, and you know that," she looked out the window, "not that you have to." Mara looked at him again. "So in my mind I ask, why would he prefer a hotel room to his home?"

"And you think Cat is the reason."

"Yes, I do. You haven't given any other reason, so what else am I to think? But you know, Jairo, I don't want to argue about it." Mara pressed her temple. "I don't. I had a great time today. It gave me a lot to think about. Obviously, you are a good man, a good human being who's done some wonderful things for others. I don't want to end the evening on this kind of a note."

"Neither do I," Jairo said. "And because what

you believe is wrong, I am inviting you to my home."

"You don't have to do this." Mara continued to press her temple.

"I want to." He started the car. "I want you to come to my house so you can see my life is not some revolving door that women come and go through. Particularly Catarina. My not wanting you to come to my home has nothing to do with her. I simply thought we might be more comfortable at the hotel. That there would be fewer interruptions since you are leaving tomorrow night." He paused. "And you are right, we don't know each other well. I am sure there is much about you that I don't know, and there are things about my life that you don't know. I thought with time these things could be revealed in a gentle manner, but perhaps I was wrong." He shook his head. "My life is not one big party, Mara. I have my troubles just like anyone else."

Mara wondered what he was trying to tell her. "I don't want my coming home with you to cause any problems."

"You don't have to worry about that."

"And Cat won't mind?"

"I don't know if she will mind or not. It's a possibility. But Catarina is not in control of my life. She is simply my stepsister."

Mara looked at him.

"That's right. Cat is my stepsister."

"Your stepsister. But she acts like—"

"And what can I do about that? I can not control her actions." Jairo pulled out into the traffic. "But I am clearing this up now. Cat is my stepsister, Mara. Her mother and my father married a long time ago. I dare say she feels my father is more of a father than I do."

"I don't know what to say," Mara replied.

"There are many things in my life, Mara, that could make you speechless." He glanced at her. "You can't look at a person and know their life."

"I didn't think I knew your entire life. I admitted that earlier. But truly, anyone would have judged from the way Catarina acted with you, touched you, that there was more."

"Well, I have set that record straight." He paused. "And considering you are leaving, it is important that we get to know each other in a deeper way."

Mara's heart quickened. "And why would we want to?"

"I would say two people who are embarking on a relationship should desire to really know who it is that they are getting involved with."

"Under normal circumstances, I would say that is true."

"So obviously, in your mind, ours is not a normal circumstance."

"Honestly speaking . . . no. I don't see it as such. You're this handsome, charming, millionaire man from Brazil. And I am a girl from Orlando, Florida. There are no adjectives to add besides I've always been smart, at least when it came to business. And I've daydreamed all my life because my life was so ordinary. It was only in my daydreams that I found excitement. So this . . . us . . . is anything but normal."

Jairo drove in silence. "Thank you for adding the man part to my description. For a second, I thought you might leave that out. You said you are a girl from Orlando, Florida. What I see is a woman, and I am a man. And that is the basic foundation for a relationship despite all the adjectives you added. And another thing that you said, that you daydream a lot, I, too, have been a dreamer. If I could not dream, Mara, I never would have made the life that you see now that is so vividly real for you and so many others. Dreaming is a powerful thing to do." He looked in the rearview mirror. "So now, we are on our way to my home. You will get to see how I live. That I do not have a wife or woman hidden in the closet." He glanced at her. "Nor does Catalina live there. But who does live there?"

Quickly, Mara looked at him.

"My father."

"You live with your father now?"

"My father lives with me," Jairo replied.

Chapter 30

Jairo pulled the Caprice up to the garage, and shut it off as the garage door descended. Mara sat awestruck by the sight of Jairo's home, a massive Mediterranean-style building.

"Only you and your father live here?"

"Basically. There are a couple of people who help around the house that stay here, but that's it."

"It's a lot of space for two, even four people, especially when I consider my living with my father in our house. It's a three-bedroom house, and when it comes to cleaning it can be a little much for me sometimes." She tried to laugh.

Jairo watched her. "Can you imagine at one point I lived here alone?"

"No-o." Mara's jaw dropped, and it was Jairo's turn to laugh.

They entered the house through what appeared to be a kind of mudroom.

"Sometimes I do have guests spending the night. They may be here because of a business deal or after a large party. Most of my guests are connected to my work, what I do. But on a personal level, if it wasn't for that, truly, Mara, I would not have a house this big. What would be the point?"

"Lord knows I'm not the one to answer that question," Mara replied.

Suddenly, a scratchy sound followed a light thud. Jairo turned abruptly. The keys that he had placed on a counter had fallen to the floor.

Mara held her heart. "Your reaction scared me more than the keys. Tell me if I'm reading you wrong, but all of a sudden you seem jumpy. It was only your keys."

He picked them up. "Yes, I see." Jairo placed them back on the counter.

"Are you sure you're not expecting some overly possessive female to jump out at any moment?" Mara chided.

He looked into her eyes. "I can only hope."

Mara gave a slight smile.

"The truth is, I thought perhaps it was my father."

"Oh, your father. So are you two pretty close now?" She asked as he led her through the kitchen.

"Not in the least," Jairo replied. "He lives here strictly because I feel a sense of duty. There is no love between us. He made sure of that when he refused to admit that I was his son when I was a child."

Mara's eyes enlarged. "That was quite a mouthful."

"We decided we were going to really get to know each other, to speak our minds. So I told you the truth, told you how it is." He turned a knob on the wall, and a soft light brightened until the room was fully illuminated.

"Oh my. This is absolutely lovely," Mara said, not having a comeback to Jairo's confession.

"I'll tell my decorators that you like it," Jairo said. "They spent lots of time turning this into what they say is a classically contemporary home. Contemporary enough so that the young people, my younger business associates, will feel comfortable, and classic enough so that the older ones won't feel out of sorts."

"But don't you like it?" Mara asked. "This is one of the most beautiful rooms I have ever been in." She looked around at the uniquely shaped couch, a matching chaise, an armless oversized chair, and what appeared to be a custom-made futon. All of the pieces were covered in high-quality fabric in gray, black, and green, with just a hint of a vibrant plum in the right places, giving what would have been drab colors sparks of life.

"I like it well enough." Jairo looked at her. "But I'm not here enough to have any feelings about it. I travel so much, Mara. I travel so-o much," he repeated with his eyes closed.

Mara walked up to him and touched his arm. "You're tired of it, aren't you, Jairo?"

"The truth is, yes, I get tired. I get real tired, but then someone like you comes along. If I hadn't traveled for tens of thousands of miles, I may never have met Mara."

Mara looked down. "You know what to say and when to say it, that . . . I'll give to you."

"Just saying what I feel, Mara. Just saying what I feel." He took her hand. "Come. Come look over here."

She followed Jairo to a sliding glass door that he

slid open effortlessly. They walked out onto a balcony that hung over a small cliff.

"How do you like this view?"

"It's breathtaking. Absolutely breathtaking," Mara replied.

"Now this, I do like. It appeals to me on every level. See there, " he stretched out his arm and pointed, "right there. You can make it out pretty well from here."

"Yes. It's the Christ with his arms stretched out. Sharon and I went to see it the other day. It's the statue that Rio is known for."

"It's called *Cristo Redemtor.* In English, Christ the Redeemer," Jairo said. "Of all the things in buying this house, to be able to see Christ the Redeemer as clearly as I see him now is the reason I bought it."

Mara looked at Jairo's face, then out at the statue that gleamed an unearthly white.

"Inside of me," Jairo continued, "my way of thinking, with the little faith that I have, I knew that no one could help me as the Christ could. So whenever I look at the statue from here, it forces me to remember that I do seek that in my life."

"Seek what?" she asked.

"Seek being restored to favor, that I have made amends."

"My . . . you sound like a man that has done quite a few things that he wants to be forgiven for."

Jairo shrugged slightly. "The truth is there is only one thing that looms in my mind, only one, and I am attempting to make amends for that, every day of my life, every day."

There was a short silence.

Mara wanted to ask Jairo what it was, but she knew it was so private, it was something that should be volunteered.

"What about you at this point in your life?" Jairo asked as they walked back inside. He closed the door. "Is there anything you are striving for deep inside of here?" His hand touched her chest and gently grazed her breasts as he removed it.

Mara inhaled, then swallowed. "Actually, there is. You got to see firsthand what is important to me."

"I did?" Jairo's brows lowered.

"The day you didn't recognize me in the conference room."

"Oh-h." He nodded, then stopped walking. Jairo placed his hands on her arms. "Mara, I'm so sorry. When I think back to that, and believe me I've thought about it many times, I don't know how that could be."

"Don't worry. It's over with now," Mara replied. "I may not have even recognized myself. I had on so much makeup I don't know if my mother would have recognized me.

"Either way, I felt really bad about that. I can never say it enough. And I was going to call you, send you some flowers, do something. But I as I told you, I got very sick."

She smiled at his sincerity. "Well, a trip to Rio for Sharon and me is probably gesture enough, so maybe I'll forgive you."

They climbed a staircase.

"But I interrupted your telling me what was your deepest desire in your life."

"Yes, you did." She took hold of his arm. "I remember that day in the conference room, you did not want to hear anything about saving those trees. Saving indigenous trees like that is my passion."

Jairo listened.

"You see," Mara continued, "ever since my mother died, I've become an advocate for the environment. Whenever I can, I try to make a difference, to help us maintain an environment that is clean and natural, to do something that keeps healthy air pumping through our lungs."

"So your attempt to save those trees had nothing to do with the Brazilian rainforest per se?"

"Not really. But I do know all rainforests are important for the well-being of the planet, and for all of us. The trees may be here in Rio, but in the circle of life everything is important, every component."

They walked through a library. Mara looked at the hundreds of books that lined the shelves. "You must be quite the reader."

"No, I'm not. But I hope that maybe my children will be. Because I am not, I want to make sure that they have all the tools that they might need to become whatever they want."

Mara stopped. "You mean, you actually think about having children, having a family?"

"Of course, I do, Mara. Of course I do," Jairo said. "Out of all the things I can tell you about growing up as a street kid, I thought one day, if I am allowed to live long enough, I will have a family. There will be a mother, a father, and children, all living together, graced with all that that brings, good and bad."

"My, my." Mara started walking again. "You are full of surprises, aren't you?"

"Why is that so surprising?" Jairo asked.

"I guess I just kind of thought a guy who would want to mow down a small plot of indigenous trees and replace them with concrete would definitely not be the kind of man who would want to put down roots and have children, creating his own family."

"See how wrong you were." Jairo turned off the lights in the library and they walked back out into the hall. "So what about your mother?" he asked softly. "Was she also someone who fought for the environment?"

"My mother?" Mara smiled. "Oh, no. No, I don't think my mother even thought about the environment. At least she never gave me any indication that she did. She was just an everyday woman. A mother doing the best she could, a woman being the best wife she could. She worked every day in a factory to try to help my father make ends meet. She didn't do anything extraordinary." Mara paused. "But I knew she loved me, and wanted for me what you want for your children." She looked at him. "And she encouraged me. She made me feel I was smart. I eventually bought into it and cultivated that part of my life."

Jairo stopped and looked down into Mara's eyes. "So what is the connection between your mother and those trees?"

"My mother died of mesothelioma," Mara replied. "It's a rare cancer caused by asbestos. And, the thing was, she didn't know that every day when she went to work to take care of me, that it was killing her. She didn't know." Mara closed her eyes. "So now I," she opened them, "try to do whatever I can to help people think about the environment, encourage them to do something about it, if they can. It's simply my way of paying my mother back for giving me life, for loving and believing in me."

"It's amazing how our motivations are so similar, Mara." Jairo inhaled and opened one of a set of double doors. "This is my bedroom." He slipped his arm around her waist. "Do you remember when I danced with you that first time at the competition?"

"Yes, I remember." Mara scanned the large room. The furniture was amazingly simple. But Mara's eyes were drawn to Jairo's face as his body pressed against her.

"I asked you why you had chosen that particular song for your dance."

"Of course, I remember."

"Well . . . out of all the songs in the world, that was my mother's favorite song, favorite tune of all tunes. No matter how bad life got, no matter how sad she was, she would hum it. And if by chance she heard it, it seemed to take her to another place."

"Really?" Mara was stunned.

He touched her lips. "I would not lie about this, Mara. And as I watched you dance with so much passion, I felt as if that music had also taken you to another place. I was transfixed as I watched you. While I lay in the hospital bed, in my heart I asked, was that a sign? How could it be, that of all the songs in the world, this woman that I am so attracted to chose the one song that my mother loved?"

"That is strange, isn't it?" Mara looked down. "I

chose it because the very first time I heard it, it sparked something inside my heart. It had a simple beauty, but underneath there was a complexity, and when I danced the samba, I wanted people to realize that's how I am." She looked into his eyes again. "And I did feel beautiful that night when I was riding around in the limousine with you. I felt like I was getting to experience some of the beautiful, extraordinary things of life." Mara looked into Jairo's eyes. "That song held the promise of all the things my life had not been until that evening of the competition. And you opened that door for me." She paused. "I have to tell you, whenever I speak of my mother I relive the grief of losing her, but I must say," she touched his face, "I can not imagine how it would feel if my mother had died when I was just a child, and to know that she was murdered." Mara shook her head. "That's beyond what I can imagine even now."

Jairo kissed her softly. "To hear that you would feel so deeply about my pain is a gift to me." He hugged her.

"I guess we couldn't have arrived in this room at a better time." Mara looked at the bed.

"I guess not," he replied.

Slowly, Mara became aware of the soft music that filled the room through hidden speakers. Jairo took hold of Mara's hand and walked over to his king-sized bed. They sat down. Mara looked out of the window across the room. She could see the moon and the fluffy clouds that floated by.

"It feels good to have you near me during your last night here. I wish that I had been able to spend more time with you, that we hadn't let silly differences keep us apart." He looked at her hands. "I like being around you, Mara. I like it a lot."

"Silly differences." She looked at his hands. "I guess they were, but at the time they didn't seem very silly to me. I was just trying to protect my heart." She touched her chest. "And no matter how easy this seems right now, I say to you again, if I'm just some kind of toy for the moment, I hope you have it within yourself to let me go back to my hotel room. If that's all I am." She looked into his eyes. "I know that wouldn't be an easy thing to do." She tried to laugh. "But still, I'm asking you as a friend, I am asking—"

"There is no way I'm going to tell you to go back to the hotel now, Mara."

"That sounds like the kind of answer that comes directly from south of the border." Her eyes turned serious. "And I'm not playing, Jairo. We're both grown enough to know that doing this again could make a difference for both of us. It could make a difference for me about how I feel about you and about myself." She swallowed." You see I'm willing to face it head on and tell the truth even as I sit here on your bed, in a house that I could only imagine in my daydreams." She held his chin. "If I am simply going to be someone you could easily forget, that won't mean anything in your life, if you like me at all, if you care for me even as a friend, you will let me walk out of here, and it will be okay."

"I've stayed away from you, Mara, for the past few days only because you told me to." He moved his face closer to hers. "Only because you told me to. It wasn't something that I wanted. Being with you is much more than a physical experience. I think you know that. I think that's why you're running scared. But I think you also know, any time you get involved with someone, if he lives in your hometown or if he lives all the way in Rio de Janeiro, you're taking a chance. But if we don't try, Mara, if we never step out of that comfort zone and try something that excites us, even if it frightens us, we've never really lived." She touched the back of her hand to his face. "So I am as clear as I've ever been about anything and anybody." Jairo put his arm around her.

"You must have your and my ability to think clearly," Mara put her hand up to her forehead, "because right now my mind is foggy and my body feels like putty. I don't think I've ever been this much of a wreck in my life about a man."

Jairo removed her hand from her forehead; then he kissed her softly on the lips. "I want you to know, Mara, how much I want you. I wanted you from the first time I saw you dance. And yes, it was physical." He put his arms around her again. "Your beauty called to me, but there was something else that I couldn't quite put my finger on. And then when I spent that evening with you I could feel something, something special. But if you are still unsure, even as I hold you in my arms, if you are still unsure, then I will do whatever you want, even if that means your leaving." But he held on to her. Mara gently pushed back. She looked into his eyes and began to unbutton her blouse.

Jairo's fingers joined hers in the task. "I'm so glad you didn't tell me that you wanted to go. I would have allowed it, but it would have been rough." He looked into her eyes, lifted her palm to his lips, and kissed it in the center. When they were both nude, Jairo kissed Mara's neck, then the tender spot between her breasts and her navel. Afterward he launched a barrage on her senses with passionate kisses.

Mara's breaths came in large bursts, which caused her breasts to rise and fall in invitation. Jairo took the bait, and licked and suckled the tips of each of the brown mounds as he caressed her waist and round hips.

"Jairo," she said softly. "I think I love you." His hand stroked her thigh and moved upward, where it found the core of her moist triangle.

In Mara's state of readiness his finger slid easily inside of her. She arched her back to receive him, and she gloried in the sensations Jairo created as he donned a condom.

"If how I feel for you is what love is, I surrender to it," Jairo said with passion. "If love can touch me so deeply that I can think of nothing but you, I have no desire to fight or run away."

He entered her throbbing and pulsing. Once there he trembled, before an overwhelming passion took over and he plunged inside her over and over again. Mara clung to Jairo as she met each of his thrusts before she exploded with intense pleasure. Moments later Jairo joined her. They remained in each other's arms until they were able to climb beneath the Egyptian cotton sheets and sleep.

Chapter 31

Mara moved between the soft cotton sheets, and as she emerged from sleep she felt as if she was emerging from a dream that was full of contentment. Slowly, she remembered where she was, and Mara opened her eyes to see a ceiling light with oblong shaped globes of various lengths. It was a work of art. Mara turned onto her side, hoping to catch Jairo in a state of sleep. Instead she saw a folded card, sitting neatly on his pillow.

Mara took it in her hand and wiped the sleep from her eyes. *Morning, wish I could be there to see how beautiful you look in the morning in my bed, but I had an early morning business meeting that could not be postponed. So wait for me, Mara. Breakfast will be brought up to you if you dial zero on the phone. JC*

Mara examined the expensive linen card before she sat up and looked around the room. With the daylight shining in, the furnishings were even more impressive. She could tell Jairo had to have a housekeeper because everything was in its place.

The only thing that made it seem more like a bedroom than a hotel room was a collection of framed photographs. Curious, Mara got out of the bed, put on a pajama top that had been placed at the end of the covers, and walked over to the photos.

It was a pictorial that stretched over several years. It wasn't difficult for Mara to pick out Jairo. In a couple of the photos he was very young. In one, he was dancing, in another he was holding a dancer's trophy. The others were group shots in which Jairo looked more businesslike than happy. The only one where there was true happiness, Mara thought, was when he was in the midst of Roberto's family with Roberto standing beside him.

Mara sat in a large armchair for awhile and thought about everything. The time she had spent in Rio, the relationship she and Jairo had begun to build, how she was in his bedroom and that he would be coming back to her. Mara took those thoughts with her when she showered and dressed. They had shared a special night, and she regretted that she would be leaving that night, but in her heart Mara felt it would not be the end of her and Jairo. Somehow they would be able to nurture their relationship.

Mara walked over to the telephone. She was about to press zero and ask for her breakfast, but suddenly she felt rather silly doing that. Mara also wondered how many women had done the same thing, and she didn't want to follow the pattern of possible female guests before her. Instead, Mara replaced the receiver and walked across the bedroom and opened the door. "I'll go downstairs into the kitchen. I'll find somebody to help me down there." She walked down the hall. "Watching them cook breakfast will be more entertaining than my sitting in Jairo's room just waiting for it to be brought to me."

Mara descended the stairs. She was surprised at how quiet the house seemed. As she got to the bottom of the stairs she tried to remember how they had reached the stairwell from the kitchen. Mara was pretty certain of her moves as she turned, entered the library, and made a right. There was a door at the end of the hall and she proceeded toward it.

"Hey. Wait a minute," a voice called.

Surprised, Mara turned. A man was standing in the hall.

"Who are you?" the man asked.

"I'm sorry. My name's Mara. I'm a guest of Jairo's." She looked at the man in his black pants and white top. "I was going to call downstairs for breakfast as he suggested, but I changed my mind." Mara walked toward him. "Could I speak to you about breakfast?"

"If you're asking if I work here," he stuffed his shirt in his pants, "I most certainly do not."

As Mara got closer she could see his red eyes, but she could see Jairo's eyes too.

"And if Jairo hasn't already told you, I'll tell you, I'm—"

"You're Jairo's father," Mara said.

He looked a little surprised.

"Yes. I am."

"I'm Mara Scott." She offered her hand. He accepted it slowly.

"I'm Benedito Flores."

"It's a pleasure to meet you, Mr. Flores."

"Just call me Benedito," he said.

"All right, and please call me Mara."

He acted as if he was about to walk away.

"Is this the way to the kitchen?" She pointed toward the door. "I really am hungry. And I didn't want to just call and have someone deliver it to my room like I was in a hotel."

"Why not?"

"Seeing that it's Jairo's home and all . . . And actually, that would be a little high on the hog for me."

"What?" His brows lowered.

"That's a southern expression. I mean I would feel a little pretentious."

"Oh." His bloodshot gaze swept her up and down.

"Plus, I was feeling a little lonely up there although Jairo has promised to come back. I didn't want to just sit there and wait."

He nodded. "Where are you from?" he asked. "No, I bet I can tell you. You are from the United States, aren't you?"

"Yes, I am. Is it that obvious?"

"It's your accent," Benedito replied.

"Accent? It's hard for me to imagine that I have an accent."

"You do," he replied.

"Obviously."

His eyes crinkled a bit, but his lips did not smile. "Come. I will show you the kitchen." He walked past her.

"Thank you," Mara replied. She wanted to say more but his demeanor did not invite it.

Moments later they entered the kitchen.

"Bernardo," he said.

A man and a woman dressed in a kind of uniform turned. They looked surprised.

"This is Mara. Jairo's guest. She's hungry. She wants some breakfast. Do you think you could make something for her?"

"Of course, Mr. Flores," the man said. They both looked at Mara.

"If you tell us what you want," the woman said, "we will be glad to prepare it."

"And I'll serve it in the dining room, if you like," the man added.

Jairo's father was about to leave the room.

"Benedito," Mara called. "Would you care to join me for breakfast?" She noted the surprised looks on the workers' faces, but Benedito's slow turn toward her gave an even clearer impression of the unorthodox nature of her request.

There was an awkward moment of silence.

"Since you are inviting me, I guess I will." He looked at the servants. "I'll take some coffee."

"Good," Mara said.

"Why don't you tell them what you want?" Benedito said.

"I'll take some toast and eggs. You can scramble them, or whatever way you cook them will be fine. And I'll have some *sucos.*" She felt proud that she remembered the word for juice.

"No coffee?" Benedito asked.

"I'd love coffee," Mara replied.

"And I'll take two pieces of dry toast. I couldn't bear to eat more than that." Benedito said. "There is a little breakfast area where I sometimes sit. Would care to eat there?"

"Sounds good to me," Mara replied.

She followed him into a small breakfast area and they sat down. There was a beautiful view outside the window.

"How long have you known Jairo?"

"Not very long," Mara said.

"I figured that."

Mara felt uneasy. "How can you tell?"

"Most of the people that Jairo knows, he makes sure that he lets them know his father, who he allows to stay in his home, is a drunk. An alcoholic. And you seem to be treating me as if you had no preconceived notions about me."

Mara was surprised again, but she hoped she didn't look it. "He's never said anything like that to me about you."

Another sparkle entered Benedito's eyes. "Truly. How about that. So we have a couple of firsts going on here."

"A couple of firsts?" Mara sat back, a little more skeptical than before.

"You're the first woman I've ever bumped into that Jairo's left here. And he didn't tell you about me, his alcoholic father. Hmmm. That makes me think a bit. Maybe he is trying to give a good impression, outside of his money."

Mara didn't know what to say, so finally she said what she was thinking. "So, why are you telling me this in such a blunt way? Are you trying to shock me?"

He sat back. "Not necessarily."

The servant entered with two empty cups and a pot of steaming coffee. He sat the cups down and filled them.

"I'm just making an observation," Benedito added.

"I see." Mara decided to be as direct. "Do you consider yourself an alcoholic?"

"I drink, yes, I do," Benedito replied.

Mara looked down, then up again. "A lot of people drink, but they don't consider themselves alcoholics."

"What does it matter? Jairo thinks I am. A lot of other people do, too. But I don't care. At this point in life, I'm going to do exactly what I want."

"I would guess from that answer you probably drink more than you need to."

Benedito simply looked at her.

"And since we're being so candid this morning, so early in meeting each other, may I ask why?"

"Why what?" Benedito asked.

"Why do you drink?"

"Oh-ho, why do I drink? That question, I have been asked by shrinks and so many other concerned individuals. Are you one of those concerned individuals?"

Mara hesitated. "I am concerned. I'm concerned about Jairo's happiness, and since you are his father and if you are drinking as much as you have indicated, then yes, I am concerned."

Benedito searched her eyes, and for the second time she could see Jairo's eyes within his bloodshot gaze.

"I believe you are concerned for the reason you said. You care about Jairo."

"Yes, I do care about your son."

"My son . . ." Benedito took a sip of coffee. "Does he know that?"

"Does he know what?" Mara replied.

"That you care about him. Has he been able to accept that?"

What a strange question. "I think so."

He smacked his hands together in mock applause before a tired look of resignation crossed his battered, handsome face. He reached in his pocket and pulled out an extremely thin flask. "Coffee just doesn't taste right without it." Clear liquid trickled from the flask into his cup.

Mara remained quiet.

Benedito took a long sip of spiked coffee. He licked his lips. "Life is strange. So strange."

Mara struggled for something to say. "Back in the States, I live with my father."

"You do?"

"Yes."

"He lives in your home?" Benedito asked.

"Oh no. It's our family home. I grew up in it with my mom and my dad. My mother died not too long ago of cancer."

"Cancer can be a slow, painful way to die."

"It was for her," Mara said quietly. "But she was a trooper to the end, and I'm grateful for the time I got to spend with her. We got to talk about all kinds of things and find what some people call closure."

"Ye-es. Closure," Benedito said. "That is important. So important. But when somebody dies abruptly, when you're not expecting them to go at all . . . no sickness. Nothing. There is no closure, and people deal with it in various ways. Jairo dealt with it by deciding he hated me. And I dealt with it in my flask." He smiled and took a long sip of coffee.

The servant returned and placed Mara's plate in front of her, and a smaller one in front of Benedito.

"But you would think, after all these years," Benedito continued, "that we would both have left it behind us. And to be fair, I guess in a way Jairo has. He found it in his heart to let me live here when I was kicked out of my own home because of drinking, and not just drinking, mind you, drinking because Jairo's mother died without closure." His eyes took on a glazed look. "But he has allowed me to be here, so I should be happy. He doesn't have to love me as a father. He doesn't have to care about me. Maybe that is more than I should expect."

Chapter 32

"How did Jairo's mother die?" Mara had to know.

"Oh, he did not tell you that either."

"No, he didn't."

"Now I'm not surprised about that." He nodded. "It's still painful for him, and I know it is because it is still painful for me. Although I'm quite sure he does not believe that." Benedito paused. "She was killed in *mata atlantica*. The rainforest that's here in Rio."

"She was murdered in a rainforest?" Mara's heart sunk. "Oh my goodness. No wonder."

"No wonder what?"

"I think Jairo's got a thing about trees or forests maybe." She looked out of the window. "Never mind," Mara continued. "Did they ever catch who did it? What was she doing there?"

"No." He shook his head like a little child, vigorously. "The people were never caught. But all these years, Jairo has blamed me because right before she went there she had found out that I had recently married and that I was not going to marry her." He sighed. "Jairo caught her crying and he made her tell him what had happened, and he was so angry at me that he told her he wanted me dead. But even then she defended me." There was pain in his eyes as he looked at Mara. "She told him never to say such things about the man who helped to give him life. That was the kind of woman Adelina was." He looked down. "Then she made Jairo promise that he would at least respect me, and never wish me harm. And she told him she wanted to be alone. She went for a walk. The next thing we knew she was found at the edge of *mata atlantica*. She had been killed."

"Poor Jairo. How old was he at the time?"

"He was nine."

"So how did he end up on the street? Why didn't he come and live with you?"

"It wasn't that simple. That's what I tried to tell Jairo. I told him that I would make it possible for him to come, but he would have to have a little patience."

"But where was he staying at that time?" Mara feared she knew the answer.

Benedito looked down. "He was living on the streets."

"And so you told a boy who had been cast out into the streets that he would have to wait until you smoothed the way for him to come? You told your son that?"

Benedito took another swig of cool coffee. "I am not proud of it. But yes, I did. I could not just force him on my wife. At the time we were newly married." His eyes pleaded for her to understand. "But by the time I had made the way for him to come—"

"He refused," Mara said.

"Yes. He preferred living on the streets to living with me."

Mara sighed. "It took quite a lot for Jairo to allow you to live here."

"Most likely it did, but it didn't have anything to do with him caring for me. He probably remembered his promise to his mother, and his image here in Rio. He's got quite the image, you know. He wants to maintain that, if nothing else."

"Well, can you blame him? That he did not rush to help you?"

"No." Benedito shook his head. "The truth is I cannot. And so, I keep it to myself, and I continue to drown it in my favorite pasttime." He drained the coffee cup, then took out the flask and drank from it directly.

"Did you love her? Did you love Jairo's mother?"

"Did I?" Benedito closed his eyes. "I loved her more than I ever loved any human being, but I could not go against my family. You see, I am not like Jairo. Jairo was born with nothing and has become a man of substance and power. And when you look at him, it looks as if it were his destiny. Me . . . I was born with a family name, but when anyone saw me, they thought of only ruin, because that was my destiny."

"Destiny." Mara looked out the window again. "I never would have believed that I would be sitting in Rio de Janeiro, at the home of a man like Jairo, and—"

"Mara?"

"Jairo." She smiled instantly as she looked at the doorway. "You're back."

He looked at her, then his father.

"I decided to come down and have breakfast," Jairo focused on her again, "instead of having it in the room all alone, and I bumped into your father. He was kind enough to show me how to get to the kitchen, so I invited him to eat with me. As you can see, he agreed."

The small breakfast area felt charged with Jairo's presence. "I can see that."

"Good morning." Benedito took a bite of toast.

"Good morning, Benedito."

Mara felt like cringing at the coldness in Jairo's voice. Instead she rattled on. "Yes, I had no idea what time you would be done, so I thought this was a good idea. And, Benedito and I have been talking."

"I overheard a bit of the conversation," Jairo said.

"How much did you hear, Jairo?" Benedito asked.

"Enough," Jairo said.

"I assume that means you heard how I said I'd never loved anyone as much as I loved your mother, Adelina."

Jairo looked out the window. "Yes. I heard you."

Benedito slapped the table. "Good. Now you know I haven't been saying it all these years for your benefit. It came from my heart, not that you believe I have one. But just for the record, I do." He got up. "And now, since Jairo is here to make your stay in Rio, however long that may be, a—"

"I leave tonight," Mara said.

"In that case, it was truly a pleasure meeting you. And it would be an honor to spend a little time with you again." Benedito raised Mara's hand and kissed it. "But it's time for me to take my leave."

Jairo stepped aside as his father approached. Benedito looked into his face. "I like her, Jairo. She's a keeper." He disappeared into the kitchen, and Jairo sat in his chair.

"How you doin'?" Mara touched his hand.

"I'm doing fine. How about you?"

"I'm great," Mara replied. "Actually, I enjoyed your father's company. He was very candid with me to say the least."

"Was he now. In what way?"

"About himself, and his drinking. And then he gave me some insight into your family."

"Really? I can't imagine what kind of insight Benedito could possibly give. I tend to question his clarity."

"And I can understand that," Mara replied. "As a matter of fact, I think he can too. I guess that's what made me feel a little sorry for him, endeared him to me just a bit."

"Oh-h," Jairo's eyebrows rose slowly.

"And Jairo, I'm really sorry to hear about your mother."

Jairo sat back. "Benedito was candid, wasn't he?"

"Yes. And with my mother being gone, if I may say so, from what he's told me, I hope one day you can find it in your heart to move on."

"Move on?" Jairo repeated.

"To forgive him for not being the father that you wanted and needed. As I listened to him talk, it wasn't because he didn't love your mother or want you in his life. I think he was afraid to stand up for what he knew was right." Mara watched Jairo's eyes slowly turn to slits. "I mean, we all have done things that we wish we could change, and sometimes it involves family."

"Really?" His voice was low.

Mara rushed on trying to make her point. "I think about my father, and I just felt through the years he's become more and more stuck in his ways. He's kind of crabby at times and sees things only one way. I've recently decided I've got to try and accept him as he is. Because, now that my mother's gone, who knows how long he will be around? We've got that in common," Mara said. "All we have is our fathers and it's important for us to love them for who they are."

Jairo remained quiet so Mara ventured a little further.

"When you think about it, what's more important?"

"I think," Jairo finally spoke, "you don't know anything about my father, my family, or the depth of what I've gone through. You have no idea what Benedito put my mother through, or how we were living one step from the street while he was going to lavish parties, and flying or cruising around the world. That's how I ended up living on the streets after my mother was killed." His eyes blazed. "Killed after Benedito told her, 'I know you are already sitting on poverty's doorstep, but no, I am not going to marry you or help you and this kid that is mine. I have just married a woman who is rich and has social status to help better myself.' "

"Jairo, I know you've been through—" She touched his hand again.

He moved it. "You have no idea. Brazil is not

America, and Rio's poverty is a far cry from Orlando's. A poor person in the United States would be well-off here. There is no way for you to understand."

Mara swallowed. "I want you to help me understand, Jairo. Help me understand."

"But you've already sought understanding from my father."

"It was only because he was candid with me. Benedito decided to tell me things that you hadn't. Not that you wouldn't have with time."

Jairo's face hardened. "I don't want to talk about this any further, Mara."

"Jairo—"

"And since you are leaving tonight, I think I should take you back to your hotel room so that you can get ready."

Mara sat and studied his expression. "Obviously, it is time for me to go." Her heart hurt. "I need to finish packing, and I'm sure by now Sharon is probably concerned about me."

Jairo's cell phone rang. He answered it and launched into a barrage of Portuguese while Mara sat uncomfortably by.

Jairo is literally putting me out. He is ready for me to go back to the hotel and back to the States. She gazed out the window and hoped her face did not betray the hurt that she felt.

"I'm sorry." He had a professional tone as he hung up the phone. "But are you ready? I do have another meeting in a little while."

"Yes, I'm ready. I'll take a taxi back."

"That won't be necessary. We'll take the limo. I'll drop you off on my way."

Mara nodded.

Mara couldn't wait for the ride back to the hotel to end. Jairo kept the conversation to safe subjects that the average tourist would be interested in knowing about Rio. Mara could have cared less. Finally, they reached the Golden Tulip, and Mara reached for the door handle as soon as the car came to a stop.

"I hope you have enjoyed your stay here in Rio." Jairo leaned over and kissed her on the cheek.

Mara closed her eyes before she managed to say, "You can believe I'll never forget it."

"Neither will I." Jairo removed a gold business card from his pocket. "Call me when you get back, so I can know you had a safe return. I do care about you, Mara."

To Mara the words were as empty as a business presentation. Mara took the card and opened the door. Before she closed it, Mara looked into Jairo's eyes. "I'm sorry if I said anything that hurt you. I'm sorry that all of a sudden you feel as if I have sided with the enemy. But Jairo, he is your father. And because he is, I wanted to like him. I wanted to know more about you, the man that had brought so much into my life so quickly. Despite of how it turned out, my intent was good." She smiled slightly. "Good-bye, Jairo." Mara closed the door and entered the hotel.

Chapter 33

8 P.M. the following night

"I'm so tired, Dad," Mara said as she got up from the couch. "I've forced myself to stay awake all day so that I could sleep tonight. I know it's kind of early, but I've got to go lie down."

"Go ahead," Nathan encouraged. "You've got to be tired after flying all night long. I'm going to read some more of the newspaper." He picked up a section from the cocktail table. "I'll see you in the morning."

"See ya," Mara replied.

She reached her bedroom and closed the door, but before she could take off her sweats, the tears began. Mara covered her face with her hands, but they were drenched in no time. Then she reached for her pillow, and with it as a buffer she allowed herself to sob. She felt as if her heart were breaking. *Jairo wouldn't let me leave like that if he really cared.* Mara felt as if she had been living a fantasy that had come to an end, but her heart didn't know it wasn't real. She sobbed into her pillow again.

"Hey, Mara," Nathan tapped on the door. "Can I show you something right quick?"

"Sure Dad. Just a minute." She dried her eyes and fanned her face in a lame attempt to get rid of some of the redness. "You can come in now."

Nathan came in with the newspaper. "Look at this." He pointed to an article about a CVS being built a couple blocks away from their house. "Ever since your mother died, you've been encouraging me to get a part-time job or something. I'm going to apply for a job here." He looked into Mara's puffy face. Slowly, Nathan lowered the paper. "You've been crying. What's wrong?"

Mara shook her head. She couldn't talk.

"Don't give me that. Something is wrong, and I'm not leaving until you tell me what it is."

"Dad . . . look, there's nothing you can do about it. I'm a big girl now, and sometimes, as we both know, life doesn't work out like we'd like."

"This has something to do with Rio?"

Mara nodded.

"You met someone over there and he did something to you." Nathan's eyes blazed. "There's international laws against this."

"No, Dad." Mara shook her head. "It's not like that." She paused. "I guess I invested my heart in a place where I shouldn't have."

"Oh-h." Nathan nodded. "I see." He kissed her damp cheek. "Well, I guess there isn't much I can do about that but give you some time alone." He walked to the doorway. "I hope you don't hurt too long, honey, because I know there is nothing like heartache."

He closed the door.

Three hours later

The telephone rang. Sleepily, Nathan reached over from his bed and answered it. "Hello."

"Hello. I'm sorry for calling so late, but is Mara there?" Jairo asked.

"Who's this?"

"My name is Jairo and I'm a friend of Mara's. She promised to call and let me know that she had a safe flight back to America, but I never heard from her."

"So you're calling here from Brazil?"

"Yes, sir. I am. Are you Mara's father?"

"Yes, I am."

"I've heard some great things about you," Jairo said.

There was silence on the line.

"It's a shame that I can't say the same about you," Nathan replied.

"Pardon?"

"Look, I don't know what happened to Mara in Brazil, but she was crying her eyes out earlier and I think you had something to do with it."

"Oh." Jairo paused. "I'm sorry Mr. Scott, I—"

"There's no need of apologizing to me. Seems like you need to apologize to her, and she's asleep now. And I'm sure, in Mara's eyes, I've already said too much, but I've got to tell you that Mara is a wonderful woman. She'd make a good wife for a good man, and if you are not going to do anything but cause her heartache, as I father I suggest you butt out now."

"To bring her heartache is not my intention," Jairo replied. "It's strange that I would be talking to you now because it was a conversation with my father that caused the problem between Mara and me."

"Oh really?"

"Yes. He told her some things that I had not had the courage to say, and because he and I don't have the best relationship, I didn't handle it well."

"Well, like I said, I've probably already said too much, but let me give you a little advice. If you care for my daughter, don't mess around with her emotions until she becomes unsure about how she feels about you. Women come to us with all the love in the world, and we take so long we just mess it up."

More silence filled the telephone line.

"And when it comes to someone you love, be it a parent, brother, sister, I don't care who it is, make sure that you do your part in building a good relationship. Time here on earth isn't guaranteed to any of us."

"I hear you, Mr. Scott." Jairo paused again. "If I asked you to do something that would help me make Mara very happy, would you?"

"Depends on what it is," Nathan replied.

"It's very simple," Jairo said, and he knew he had an ally.

Chapter 34

"Hey, Mara."

Mara looked up from the couch. "Hey, Dad."

"Thought if you can put aside your jet lag long enough, you might want to get a bite to eat with Helen and me."

Mara studied her Dad's face. It looked more youthful than it had in a long time. "Sure. I'll come."

"Good," he replied.

"From this can I assume that you and Helen are getting along pretty well?"

"You may definitely assume that." Nathan pulled his pants up by the belt.

Mara smiled. "You don't believe in mincing words, do you, Dad?"

"What's the point? I've always been a direct man. Your mother could have vouched for that."

"So can I," Mara replied.

Nathan looked at his watch. "Dinner at Chili's is

set for seven, so we'll go and pick Helen up at six-
thirty."

"It's a date." Mara watched her father walk away.
She started to turn back to the television, but
something stopped her. "Dad?"

"Uh-huh?"

"I'm glad that you like Helen. It makes a difference when you find somebody that you're compat-
ible with."

"It does," Nathan replied. "You know your
mother and I had a great relationship all those
years. And for a while I thought I had to forget it,
let go of what we had in order to let someone else
into my life." He smiled. "But Helen helped me
see that life is for the living, and that I could still
be with her and treasure what Janet and I shared.
Sometimes old feelings and ways die hard, but
there's still hope. Yep." He nodded. "I think Helen
will be a good person to have in my life."

Mara looked down. "That's quite a lesson to
learn."

His eyes sparkled. "And I recently found out
that I'm not the only one who has struggled with
something similar." Again Nathan turned to walk
away.

"And Dad."

"Yeah?"

"I'll be going back to work in a week. I start next
Monday. I got a call from my headhunter. She
found me another project."

"Good. I knew that she would. I wasn't worried
in the least."

Mara tried to keep a straight face.

Nathan walked away again. "Be ready no later

than ten after six because I want to pick Helen up at six-thirty."

"I'll be ready," Mara replied.

They pulled up in front of Helen's house at six-thirty. Mara climbed into the backseat and allowed her father's new friend to sit beside him. She listened at their easy, everyday chatter. Mara couldn't remember when she'd heard her father laugh so much, and she was happy for him.

As she gazed out the back window, Mara couldn't help but think about Jairo. She'd been back in the States for three days. Mara had not called him, at least not yet, and he had not called her.

She watched the people on the streets and the cars that drove by. Earlier, Sharon had called and said she and Roberto had plans for the evening. To Mara it seemed things were working out for everyone but her. James flashed through her mind, but there was no desire to call him at all. James, who didn't see her as sexy or desirable. Mara's mouth formed a sad smile. Perhaps she should thank James for breaking up with her. It made her step out and see herself in a different light. And then she thought, perhaps she should thank Jairo as well for allowing her to know how passionate she could be, how easily and deeply she could love. "Even if I never see him again."

"Say what?" Nathan asked.

"Huh?" Mara replied.

"I thought you said something."

"You know me, Dad. I guess I was talking to myself."

"Here we are." Nathan pulled up into the Chili's parking lot.

They climbed out of the car.

"So I understand," Helen said as Mara walked beside her and Nathan, "you just got back from your trip."

"Yeah. I've been back for a couple of days. I'm not quite over my jet lag, but I'm adjusting."

"You went to Brazil, right?"

Nathan opened the door for both of them.

"Yes. Rio de Janeiro."

Helen rolled her eyes toward the ceiling. "I can only dream of going someplace like that."

"Maybe we'll have to work on making that dream come true," Nathan said.

"Really?" Helen's smile made her look ten years younger.

"With a little time, I feel like I might be up to making a big trip," Nathan said. "But I'll need to practice with a few smaller ones." He grinned.

Mara couldn't believe it.

Helen slipped her arm through his. "Well, if you decide to go, you definitely have a traveling buddy."

Nathan and Helen smiled and looked at each other as they waited for the woman who was doing the seating. It was only a matter of minutes before they were sitting in a booth looking over the menu that was more than a little familiar to Mara.

"I think I'm going to try one of those big margaritas that they serve," Helen said.

"At this time of day?" Nathan asked.

"Why not? It's evening, isn't it?" Helen replied.

"Yes, but . . ."

"But what?" She looked at him.

He squeezed her hand. "That's right, but what? Helen, you go ahead and enjoy yourself. Life is too short not to. As a matter of fact, I think I'll have a beer."

Mara smiled. She thought about joining Helen with a margarita. It might help her sleep a little better than she slept the night before.

"Oh, by the way," Nathan said, "here. This is something that came for you." He placed an envelope in front of Mara.

She looked at the writing on the outside. She didn't recognize it, and there was no return address. "How did it get here?"

Nathan shrugged.

Mara opened it. There was a note card inside, and on the exterior was an image of Jairo's project that she had worked on. "Why, this is . . ." Mara studied the goldlike lithograph drawing. Then she realized everything was gold except for the trees, the indigenous trees were there, and they were a subtle but distinct green. Mara brought the notecard closer to her face as she read a plaque that was positioned in front of them. "The Mothers." She looked at her father. "What is this, Dad?"

"Don't ask me. Why don't you ask him?"

Mara turned, and there stood Jairo in some jeans and a deep blue T-shirt. "Jairo! What are you doing here?"

"Your father invited me."

Jairo sat down beside Mara. When she looked at her father and Helen, they both smiled.

Nathan began to laugh. "Now, I like this. The last time I was able to pull the wool over your eyes you were a little girl. You had such an imagination then. You'd believe anything."

"Well, you did it this time," Mara replied as Jairo put his arm around her.

"And it is all your father's fault," Jairo said. "I called you the other night and I got your father on the phone. So just like you had a talk with my father, I talked with yours. We talked for quite a while. And it was after I spoke to him that I realized if I was going to be able to pursue our relationship, I was going to have to really let go of the pain and the anger I had been carrying around for years. And because of my love for you, Mara, I've done just that."

"Oh Jairo." Her eyes filled with tears.

Dear Reader,

This is simply a letter of thanks for the support you have shown me through the years. How blessed I have been to share my imagination and my dreams through the pages of my novels. You have accompanied me on my spiritual journey, and I hope that no matter where I go you will always be with me. Whether it is through romantic adventure, mainstream fiction or through nonfiction Eboni Snoe, Gwyn Ferris McGee will always carry you in her heart.

Keep a Smile in Your Heart,
Eboni Snoe

ABOUT THE AUTHOR

Eboni Snoe broke new ground with her debut novel, *Beguiled*, becoming one of the original and best-known writers in the African-American romance genre. She is an award-winning author of six Arabesque novels. She travels extensively to exotic destinations and currently resides in Salt Lake City, Utah.

BOOK YOUR PLACE ON OUR WEBSITE AND MAKE THE ARABESQUE ROMANCE CONNECTION!

We've created a customized website just for our very special Arabesque readers, where you can get the inside scoop on everything that's going on with Arabesque romance novels.

When you come online, you'll have the exciting opportunity to:

- View covers of upcoming books

- Learn about our future publishing schedule (listed by publication month and author)

- Find out when your favorite authors will be visiting a city near you

- Search for and order backlist books

- Check out author bios and background information

- Send e-mail to your favorite authors

- Join us in weekly chats with authors, readers and other guests

- Get writing guidelines

- AND MUCH MORE!

Visit our website at
http://www.arabesquebooks.com

Put a Little Romance in Your Life With

Louré Bussey

__**Dangerous Passions** 1-58314-129-4	$5.99US/$7.99CAN
__**Images of Ecstasy** 1-58314-115-4	$5.99US/$7.99CAN
__**Just the Thought of You** 1-58314-367-X	$5.99US/$7.99CAN
__**Love So True** 0-7860-0608-0	$4.99US/$6.50CAN
__**Most of All** 0-7860-0456-8	$4.99US/$6.50CAN
__**Nightfall** 0-7860-0332-4	$4.99US/$6.50CAN
__**Twist of Fate** 0-7860-0513-0	$4.99US/$6.50CAN
__**A Taste of Love** 1-58314-315-7	$5.99US/$7.99CAN
__**If Loving You Is Wrong** 1-58314-346-7	$6.99US/$9.99CAN

Available Wherever Books Are Sold!

Visit our website at **www.BET.com.**

More Sizzling Romance From
Francine Craft

__Betrayed by Love	1-58314-152-9	$5.99US/$7.99CAN
__Devoted	0-7860-0094-5	$4.99US/$5.99CAN
__Forever Love	1-58314-194-4	$5.99US/$7.99CAN
__Haunted Heart	1-58314-301-7	$5.99US/$7.99CAN
__Lyrics of Love	0-7860-0531-9	$4.99US/$6.50CAN
__Star-Crossed	1-58314-099-9	$5.99US/$7.99CAN
__Still in Love	1-58314-005-0	$4.99US/$6.50CAN
__What Matters Most	1-58314-195-2	$5.99US/$7.99CAN
__Born to Love You	1-58314-302-5	$5.99US/$7.99CAN

Available Wherever Books Are Sold!

Visit our website at **www.BET.com**.